MURDER AT TWILIGHT

FLEUR HITCHCOCK

For the Children of Abbots Worthy

First published in the UK in 2018 by Nosy Crow Ltd
The Crow's Nest, 14 Baden Place
Crosby Row, London, SE1 1YW

1 3 5 7 9 10 8 6 4 2

A CIP catalogue record for this book is available from the British Library

Printed and bound in Great Britain by Clays Ltd, Elcograf S.p.A.
Typeset by Tiger Media

Papers used by Nosy Crow are made from wood grown in sustainable forests.

ISBN: 978 1 78800 062 8

www.nosycrow.com

Prologue

I'll start at the beginning, because that's what you're supposed to do.

Although that would be me falling in the river when I was two and him falling in afterwards because he thought I was waving, not drowning. That was the first time I met him.

Apparently.

No, I'll start at the second beginning.

The one before where it all kicked off.

That one.

Chapter I

Mum and I are having the same row we always have. About changing the way we live. I want to change everything; she doesn't want to change anything.

"For goodness', sake, Viv!" says Mum, lobbing her tea bag into the sink. "There's no point in you taking the bus. I'm already driving past your school on the way to Noah's!" She bangs her mug on to the kitchen table. "And that – is that. Now, are you ready?"

"Why doesn't Noah take the bus too?"

Mum doesn't answer.

"Because he's too precious – that's why, isn't it?"

"Stop it, Viv. It's all hard enough without you –" Mum shakes her head from side to side, "making it worse."

Tai, our dog, yaps and dances around the table legs. He thinks we're playing.

Too angry to even stroke him, I yank up my tights and jam my feet into my battered school shoes without undoing the laces. It's always like this. We always please them. We're always going to have to *fit in* with the Belcombes. Because Mum was Noah's nanny. Mum wiped baby Noah's bottom, read baby Noah his bedtime stories, patched up baby Noah's cuts and bruises. She still drives him to school, buys his clothes, makes him practise the violin. Noah is Mum's job. I'm – well, I'm me.

I shoulder my school bag.

And he's super precious because he's the last of the family line. There isn't another one. Noah Nathaniel Simeon Belcombe, only child, otherwise known as Viscount Alchester, is first in line to the family throne. He's an endangered species.

I'm plain old Vivienne Lin.

I crash through the kitchen door, letting it slam back against the wall, and stomp down the stone steps into the leaves swirling around the main courtyard.

"But you didn't even touch your toast!" shouts Mum behind me.

At the top of the steps Tai tilts his head to one side, looking hopefully at my breakfast sagging in Mum's hand.

I don't answer.

"Viv! You'll be starving by lunchtime."

I still don't answer.

Behind me, Mum sighs.

"Bye, Tai," she says, closing the door to our little flat above the old stables and sweeping past me to the shiny green Mini parked on the gravel in front of the main house. Lights flash and the Belcombes' third car makes a smug little electronic bleep as she unlocks it.

"Get in, please, Viv," she mutters.

I lean on the front passenger door and slowly her eyes come up to meet mine. "Back seat, please, Viv. Now, please."

I stay put, conscious that defiance is making me tremble slightly, and I wait, still leaning on the outside of the car, while she lets herself into the big house and comes out a moment later, followed by Noah, gleaming in his dry-cleaned St David's uniform, his new shoes polished, his blond curls brushed into a golden froth.

"Morning, Noah," says Mum, pulling a tight smile.

"Morning, Marion," he says, coming round to the front of the car and nudging me out of the way, before yanking the door open and throwing his school bag inside. Following the bag, he squeezes himself into the front seat and immediately starts to fiddle with the stereo.

"I wonder," says Mum, standing at the driver's door. "I wonder if you two could manage a journey, together, in the back?"

"What?" says Noah, his stupid forelock of curls flopping over his face. "But I always sit in the front!"

"You do at the moment," says Mum, super calmly, "but you didn't used to – if you remember, it's only been a month … since you…" She stops.

"Since you threw my bag out of the window on the main road," I add, my arms tightly folded. "And didn't get out to pick it up, and didn't apologise."

"Viv," snaps Mum. "So I thought we could return to the way it was before. The two of you together, getting on nicely in the back." She hesitates. "It's fairer."

Part of me wants to whoop with joy. Mum, standing up for my rights over the little lordship, holding a valiant flag up against the tyranny of the family that has everything. And part of me wants to climb into the boot and sit in the dog hairs to avoid sitting next to him.

He's a bully and I don't want to share a seat.

If he could disappear, right here, right in front of me and Mum – I wouldn't shed a single tear. I'd laugh.

"No," he says, clicking his seatbelt across his chest. "No. I won't."

Mum's jaw drops open.

"Noah Belcombe. Would you please sit in the back of the car so that Viv can sit next to you. Please."

He gets out his iPhone and starts to swipe through his photos.

"Don't worry, Mum. He's just a pig – an inbred pig," I say, walking round to the driver's side and pulling the seat forward. "I wouldn't sit next to him if you paid me."

Noah swings round as I'm about to get into the

seat behind him. "Take that back, you little –" And he lunges for my hair.

I've got faster reactions than him – always have had – and I thrust my hand out to stop him, but the outer side of my palm connects with the underside of his nose.

"Ow!" He yowls and blood explodes across the car.

"Oh, god! Viv – Noah – stop it!" says Mum, reaching for tissues.

But actually, I don't want to stop it and I punch Noah's nose just a little bit more, so that the blood sprays down the front of his trousers.

Mum jumps into the front seat and closes the door. I don't think she wants Noah's parents to see what's going on in the car, although in the last ten years we've had some pretty spectacular fights – and she can't have kept them all hidden.

"Oh, no." She dabs at him with kitchen roll that she finds in the glove compartment. "Oh, Viv – you idiot."

"Not my fault," I say, settling back, feeling horrible mixed emotions about Mum scrabbling to clean Noah's face balanced with enormous satisfaction in having caused him so much discomfort.

"You're dangerous, you are!" Noah splutters, pinching the top of his nose to stop the blood.

Mum looks anxiously at the fall-out. A mass of bloody tissues and kitchen roll bounce across the car. Noah's white shirt is still white, but his jacket has dark marks on it; his bag too. "It's not too bad," she says, starting the car and rolling gently out of the drive. "It'll stop in a minute."

"Not bad – I should call the police on you!" he says, jabbing his finger in my direction.

"Oh, yeah," I say. "Like calling someone inbred when they come from one of the most inbred families in the world is wrong? I'm just being scientific. The gene pool in your ridiculous family must be—"

"Shut up, Viv," barks Mum. "And apologise."

"I didn't do anything," I say, crossing my arms and staring out of the window. "He started it. He wouldn't share."

"Silence! Both of you!" yells Mum as we pull out on to the road.

No one speaks as we glide through the woods down the long, long drive. Connor Evans, the gamekeeper, is stoking a bonfire on the edge of the grass and he waves at us. None of us wave back. I would, but honestly, I'm too angry. Mum pauses as the electric gates open and we pull out into the lane, leaving the Blackwater Estate behind. The village flashes past and soon we're in the suburbs of Alchester. Mum negotiates the traffic and still we sit in silence, listening to the *tick-tick* of the indicators. Noah texts me.

I'll get you later, he says.

In your dreams, troll I text back.

And the beginning of the chain-link fence that surrounds my school appears on our right.

We approach Herschel High and Mum pulls into the usual lay-by, leaps out and tips her seat forward. Without a word to Noah, I clamber out.

"Bye, Mum," I say, turning my back on the car and walking into school, ears burning, face burning, everything burning.

Chapter 2

I'm still furious when I bump into Nadine, Sabriya and Joe by the bus shelter. Nadine takes one look at my face and says, "Noah?"

"He's a…" I can't actually think of a word.

"An amoeba," says Joe.

"A slug," says Sabriya.

"A school sausage roll, with school gravy," says Nadine.

"A school-mash-and-roast-beef smoothie," says Joe, and they laugh. Although I don't, because inside, I seem to have lost my sense of humour.

"Yes," I say. "He is. He's all of those things."

We join the living stream of Herschel High students pouring in through the gates. The two-minute bell rings.

"Hey, Viv, you've got ketchup or ink or something on your hand," says Joe as we spill into the corridor.

"Oh! Yuk." I wipe it off on my bag. "It's Noah's blood. I actually punched him."

Sabriya raises her eyebrows. "Noah's blood – for real?"

I nod. "Yup," I say, a blush racing up my face. "And he bled like a … a…"

"…pig?" suggests Joe, shoving me towards my tutor room, just as the bell begins to ring.

* * *

"Vivienne Lin!" calls Miss Parker.

"Here," I say.

She marks me down in the register and I look at my timetable. Double Maths next. OK, I can do this. I'm not bad at maths, and if I want to become an architect, I've got to get a good grade. If I could just get Noah out of my head and start breathing properly everything would be fine.

I peek down at my bag. There's the dark stain from his blood. I wish I'd spotted it earlier – I could have washed it off before Tutor.

Mindfulness – isn't that what they call it? I stare out of the window. Autumn sunlight streams through towards me, blinding me. I try to concentrate on the little scraps of dust floating in the sunbeams. I try to control my breathing but an image of Noah's curly blond hair, catching the sunlight, creeps into my mind. The hair thing's always happened, and when we were little, all the adults would go *ahhhh. How sweet,* and then they'd look at me sideways and say, *I bet she's clever.*

Well, I am. I'm cleverer than him, I always have been, and I haven't had any of his advantages. For a start, I'm here at crummy old Herschel High – not perfect St David's. I'm plain old Vivienne Lin, he's Viscount Alchester – lord-of-the-manor-to-be. Then there's the squillions of acres and the whole feudal thing of everyone treating you like a lord. It's like a place that got stuck. No one can ever leave working there because they live in houses that belong to the Belcombes and there are no other houses to live in because the Belcombes own everything for miles. It's like everything you ever earn goes back to the people you earn it from. I've heard them all complaining, especially the people with large families to support – they have to rent bigger cottages, which means more rent, less money left over. That's why I want to be an architect and build affordable housing for me and for others. And I want to build my own modern house on my own patch of land. I want to be my own person.

My mindfulness has flown straight out of the window and I look down at the bloodstain on my bag. I wonder if his nose is still sore? I feel a slight twinge of guilt. Very slight. Noah does get nosebleeds. Always has. But they've mostly been to do with altitude, not fists. Examining the back of my hand for spatter, I think of all the blood shooting out across the car – there was a lot. It was spectacular.

The bell rings and we fill the corridors, queuing to get into lessons, blocking the doorways. To get to Maths I'm going to have to go past the toilets, so I rush along the corridor and dive into the ladies', running my bag under the cold tap and washing my hands with a thick glob of pink goo soap. It takes minutes rather than seconds so I get into Maths after everyone's sitting down.

"Nice to see you at last, Vivienne," says Mr Marlow, swinging in his chair, arms raised above his head revealing two perfect circles of sweat on his checked shirt. I try not to look, or sniff, but can't help myself and begin to laugh as the stale sweat reaches me. Maths is hard enough without this.

"Can we open the window, sir?" I ask.

"Just sit down, please, Vivienne," he says, leaning forward and clunking his chair.

"But," says Sonny next to me, "it's really hot in here, sir."

"Yes, sir," says Juliet. "I can hardly breathe."

"Yes, sir – it's like, boiling in here," says someone.

"So stuffy," says someone else.

"Can we at least take off our jackets?"

"Sit down, please, Vivienne, and quiet, everyone," says Mr Marlow, his arms down, the offending armpits out of sight, but not out of smell.

"But, sir," I say. "Windows, please, sir – or we won't be able to concentrate."

Mr Marlow stands and points at the clock. "I've wasted seven minutes of my life waiting for you lot to be lesson ready," he says. "Seven minutes. That's seven minutes I won't get back." He sits on top of his desk and taps his fingers against the side.

"And I've wasted seven minutes of mine breathing

in your stinking armpits," I whisper, slightly too loud in the sudden silence.

* * *

I don't really mind detention. Apart from anything else it means I won't be stuck in the car going home with Noah. I text Mum to tell her I won't be ready on time and she texts back an emoji of a bus.

Fair enough.

Today, we're litter-picking with Señora Delgado. She's actually lovely and when I tell her how I ended up in detention, she laughs. "Oh, you are so naughty, Vivienne. Poor Mr Marlow."

But because detention overruns, I miss the late school bus.

That means I'm going to have to walk into the centre of town. And catch the ordinary bus home.

And the beautiful sunlight that's been streaming all day suddenly fades, and it feels like winter and I wish that I'd eaten the toast Mum made, or grabbed my bobble hat or gone home at normal time in the car.

A police car screams down the road towards St David's.

Shivering, I clutch my jacket across my chest and hunch up my shoulders. There isn't much wind but it feels as if there is, and the cold creeps in through my neck and my cuffs and everywhere. Tights just aren't enough protection when the temperature's plummeting and my legs turn to lumps of ice.

By the time I reach the bus station, I'm frozen.

I get out my phone and send Mum a text to say I'll be on the next bus, but she doesn't reply.

Then I send Nadine a photo of my frozen feet.

She sends me one of her feet in slippers on her duvet.

I send her one of the scary woman in pink sitting on the line of chairs.

She sends me one of her cat.

I send her a selfie of my head against the announcement board.

She sends me one of a cheese toastie.

The bus comes and I have to wait while thousands of people with bus passes fill all the easy seats.

I sit at the very back and slowly warm up as the bus wanders through the edge of town. Then the house lights fade away and it's just cold countryside out there.

We stop in Easton Abbas. An old woman with a trolley slowly shuffles to the front of the bus and gets out. She vanishes in the gloom and the bus pulls away, lunging through potholes, speeding around the bends in the road, and tossing me back and forth along the back seat until I feel sick. Finally we rumble into Blackwater Abbas, where I ring the bell and lurch down the middle towards the door. No one else gets off and I'm surprised to see the reflective strip of a police car caught in the bus headlights as it slips past. There are never any police around here. Nothing ever happens.

I wait as the bus pulls away, the roar of the engine and the glow of the rear lights vanishing in the direction of Lower Marston. Pulling up the collar of my jacket, I run past the few houses and along the footpathless lane as far as the gates of Blackwater House. There are no lights, but I'm used to this road in total darkness. And it isn't totally dark, there's a candy sunset streaking the western sky. Reaching the gates, I stop and punch in the entry code. With a groan they open and let me through.

An owl hoots.

The light from my phone seems over-bright as I text Mum.

Any chance of a lift from the gates?

But there's no answer, so I try ringing. Again, no

answer. It goes to voicemail straight away. That's odd. Mum keeps her phone switched on all the time. In case of Noah. He may not be four any more, but he still seems to need her holding his hand.

She's probably helping him with his homework. Or taking his jacket to the dry cleaners.

Putting my phone back in my inside pocket, I pause for a moment, listening to crunching noises all around me. At first I can't work out what they are, and then I realise they must be ice crystals forming. My jacket has no more warmth to give. No amount of dragging it across my chest is going to make any difference, and the pockets are stupid not-real ones so all I can do is jam each hand inside the cuff of the other sleeve and clutch my arms across my chest. It's like wearing a cold straitjacket.

Off to my right are the glowing remains of Connor's bonfire, and for a moment I stand with my toes in the ash, hoping the feeble embers might do something to warm me up.

They don't.

Right now, I'm kind of regretting that detention. I could have come home with Mum and Noah in the Mini. Instead, there's the whole drive to walk.

Though – I glance off to the left – there are the bushes; I could take a short cut. Leaving the fire and brushing through the beech hedge, I strike out over the lumpy verge where there's a kind of badger footpath. The ground crunches under my feet and when I look up at the sky it's perfectly clear and there's a star already twinkling. It's going to be seriously cold tonight.

The hedge closes behind me and I navigate using the tops of the trees silhouetted against the greeny-orange sky. There are fewer of them to the right, which must be the path to get to the house. Although I'm fairly sure of my way, branches thwack against my face and drag at my clothes. It's been some time since I tried to come through here and I wonder if I'm going to walk into a wall of brambles. I must have been with Noah last time. It must have been one of our getting-on moments. I'd convinced him that there was a ghost living here, in the drive woods. We sat for hours waiting one night until a badger appeared and spooked us. We ran home screaming.

As I approach the house I'm met by flashing blue lights. Police? Here?

Three squad cars fill the courtyard outside

the house and there are some massive lamps floodlighting the Mini. People in white all-over suits are rummaging inside and underneath it. They've set up a white plastic gazebo and the lights are so strong it looks like a film set.

"What's going on?" I say to the air.

This is not normal.

Chapter 3

No one seems to notice me, and I pause at the entrance to the courtyard, trying to decide whether I should go up to our flat or talk to a police person or try the doors of the big house.

In the end, I decide to try the flat. The door's unlocked, it's nice and cosy, but there's no sign of Mum. Instead, Tai bounces up to me, his tail wagging. He yaps and trots over to the back door so I let him out down the back steps to wee in the stable yard.

"What's going on, Tai?" I ask, resting my hands on the radiator. "Why are the police here?" He answers by squeezing back in through the gap in the door, rolling on to his back and squirming around until I rub his tummy. "And where's Mum?"

Flipping back on to his feet, he examines his empty food bowl, prodding it with his nose and making sad noises. Eventually, he pushes it right across the floor and looks up at me. Hopeful.

"You haven't been fed?" I say, finding half an open tin of dog food in the fridge. It looks like the same tin of food Mum opened this morning. "You really haven't been fed – you must be starving." Prising the lid open I spoon out the disgusting jellied lumps. "Here."

Tai snuffles around me and makes extravagant eating sounds. I rub his ears and the food vanishes in seconds. "What have you done with Mum, eh?"

While he licks the bowl clean I wander over to the little window next to the front door and peer out through the slatted blind into the courtyard. I don't think anyone can see me, so I watch for a few minutes, trying to make sense of everything. The people in white are very busy sticking things into bags, and one of them is crawling across the tarmac on their hands and knees with their nose about an inch above the ground.

If it wasn't really disturbing it would be funny.

As I stare out, the front door at the top of the steps to the main house opens, and framed in a rectangle of orange light is Sharon, Chris the waterkeeper's girlfriend. She's looking down at her phone, so I can't really see her expression because she's got this long blonde hair that hangs down in a sheet on either side of her head. Behind her comes Dave McAndrew, the man from the sawmill, and Connor Evans, the gamekeeper, both looking worried. They're followed by Lord Belcombe and Chris himself. They all bundle into the Land Rover and sweep out of the courtyard.

Then Lady Belcombe, Noah's mum, appears at the top of the steps, watches the white-suited people for a moment, checks her phone and goes back inside, without closing the door properly.

"What shall I do, Tai?" I ask, stepping back from the window.

In answer, Tai lies down, crosses his paws and rests his head on my foot.

"I need to do something, I can't just stand here waiting." I don't usually go into the main house, but I really want to find out what's happened – and if anyone asks, I'll say I'm searching for Mum, which I kind of am.

A little bit terrified, I run down our steps, cross the courtyard and walk up the grand marble steps that lead to the house. I know Lord B's out, I saw him go, but Lady B's not easy. Mum's very good with her but she can be scary, mostly because she's used to people following her orders. She ran a newspaper or something before becoming a Belcombe. She doesn't fit here in the middle of the countryside. I don't think I've ever seen her outside unless the sun's shining. She's too towny and she probably knows it. Maybe that's why she's so prickly. Perhaps country people make her feel uncomfortable.

Or am I kidding myself?

The heavy oak door swings open as I touch it and I stick my head around. It gives straight on to the hallway – which is really a giant open barn thingy, as big as most people's whole houses, with a fireplace, sofas and a table. Portraits of ancient Belcombes line the walls and the corners of the room disappear in polished wood murk.

Lady Belcombe is standing in front of the fireplace, her face streaked with tears. When she sees it's me she rushes forward to grab my arm.

"Vivienne, darling, I'm so glad you're back. Have you heard anything from little Noah? Have you seen him? He hasn't come home, he wasn't there when Marion went to pick him up, and…" She shakes her head as if there's something more she's not going to tell me. "I'm so worried about him."

"What?" I say. "Mum went to pick him up from school and he wasn't *there*?" I try to keep the excitement out of my voice. This is thrilling on many levels.

"He's vanished," she says, sniffing. "Has he contacted you?"

I reach for my phone. "No," I'm saying already. "No – not as far as I know, nothing." I hold it up. Apart from this morning's *I'll get you later*, the last message from Noah was six months ago, when he'd sent me the charming words, *Suck it up, loser*.

That probably marked the absolutely final end of our not very beautiful friendship.

"Vanished – like, disappeared?" I say. She's not listening to me though.

A policewoman comes out of the sitting room and takes Lady B by the elbow. "Shall I make you another cup of tea?" she asks.

"I've had enough of tea, you stupid woman,"

Lady B snaps, and then, as if remembering that she's talking to a police officer, she says, "No, no thank you very much," sniffs and sinks into one of the monumental leather sofas, trembling and blowing her nose. "Vivienne, sit down and help this woman find my son." She points at the other vast sofa, one that must have seen the death of several cows.

Ignoring everyone, Tigger, the Belcombes' cat, struts over and wipes his head on my shin then sits and licks his chest. I bury my hand in the thick fur behind his head and try to feel normal. Because she's told me to, I sit down, but it feels surreal sitting here with Lady B and the cat.

"Ah – Vivienne? Vivienne Lin." Not at all bothered by Lady B, the policewoman checks a notebook. "You live here, don't you?" she says. "We need to talk to you."

"What's happened to Noah?" I ask. "Where's my mum?" Tigger leaps from the floor and settles on my lap, purring.

"Your mother? Oh, yes, she's showing one of my colleagues the route she took to St David's this morning. As for Noah, we're just checking every avenue at this stage." The policewoman delivers a glowing smile. "As you're sitting down, would you like to talk here? Just an informal chat. We're trying to establish one or two things about him – his interests, that sort of thing."

Of course I'll answer questions. Anyway, I don't suppose I have much choice.

The policewoman perches on the arm of the sofa. It's probably meant to make her seem informal, but she looks awkward in these surroundings. Everything in this room is carefully ancient. Wood panelling, blazing logs, long oak table, battered leather sofas, an heirloom rug casually covering most but not all of the smooth old floorboards. Even the greyhound lying in the firelight, her head on her forepaw, is medieval.

The policewoman, however, looks like she came from IKEA – clothes all dayglo and orange, and modern and functional. She, me and Tigger are all out of place. I grip the cat tighter.

"So, tell us about Noah." She leans forward and her dayglo creaks. "What did you and Noah do together, mostly? I gather you're the same age."

"Do together?" I shrug. "Well, nothing, any more. He goes to a different school, has different friends – although I don't know if he actually has any friends."

"Oh?" The policewoman looks up from her notebook. "How would you know? If you don't have much to do with each other?"

Looking out, I see lights moving around in the garden. Perhaps I'm imagining them. This is all so weird. I think about my answer instead. How *would* I know?

"I've just never seen any here. My friends come back for sleepovers and stuff. He doesn't…" I tail off, conscious of Lady B turning slightly towards us, "…seem to do that sort of thing."

Outside, the police people are talking together. An engine starts. More lights flash through the windows. Lady B gets to her feet and then sits down again; she checks her phone, and checks it again.

The policewoman is writing. In the silence, Lady Belcombe's sniffing seems really loud, as does the crackling of the fire. Tigger stretches down and settles across my feet.

"Why is Mum helping you? When did Noah disappear?"

"All in good time." The policewoman fixes a smile that tells me nothing. "What about his relationship with sport? Rugby in particular."

"I've no idea," I say. "He's not – I mean we used to climb trees and ride bikes and that..."

"How about people – were there any people he mentioned?"

"I said about the friends..." I glance over to Lady B, who is still sniffing on the sofa, but definitely listening.

"No – more like teachers. Did he ever say anything about any teachers? At all?" The policewoman looks up into my face and stares really hard.

I shrug. I shake my head. "No – no, I've no idea."

"Perhaps it's just coincidence," she says, with no explanation. "Was there anywhere that might be special to Noah? You know, a hiding place?" She leans forward conspiratorially. It doesn't work, she's still like a teacher. But then I remember that this is Noah and I don't owe him anything. I owe this policewoman more. I try to think of what he might do – where he might hide. *Would* he hide? He would have done when he was six, but I don't really know the twelve-year-old Noah.

I shake my head as I try to remember all the places that we hung out as kids. "The shed on the river? Where the waterkeepers kept all their stuff

– they call it The Palace. We used to try to get in, but old Mr Mumford always chased us away. There was the big walnut tree in the middle meadow, we almost killed each other there." I glance over to Lady B. She's listening, her brow furrowed as if she's imagining all the places that I'm talking about. "The yew tree by the chalk pond? I think he defended it and I threw fir cones at him. We both built fortresses all over the gardens – even in the ditches by Long Wood..."

The policewoman looks up at me. "Always at war?"

I nod. "Definitely."

She sits back and pings her glow-in-the-dark tabard thingy. "So he could be anywhere?"

"S'pose so. But it's very cold."

I don't think I'm the only one that jumps when the front door swings open and Lord Belcombe steps in, followed by Connor Evans, Dave McAndrew, Pavel, one of the part-time gardeners, and two policemen. They bring in the cold and they all look grim. They looked worried before, but now, behind his beard, Dave McAndrew is white – sheet white – and he sees Lady B, tearful on the sofa, and turns away from her as if he can't bear it.

"We really have searched everywhere," mutters Lord Belcombe to his wife, who launches into another wave of sobbing. "Just now we tried the pheasant hatchery, and the smokery, just in case, but no joy. Tony and Shona are still out checking the gardens. They might find him – if he's hiding."

I look out at the lights moving around in the dark. Ah – the gardeners with torches.

"But why would he be hiding? The poor little..." Lady B launches into a new round of sobbing.

Lord B sits down next to his wife, still wearing his waxed jacket and walking boots, and takes one of her hands in his. "It'll be all right," he says, but underneath his wild curly hair his sad face and worried eyes say that he doesn't believe it himself.

For a moment, I feel sorry for him.

Connor and Pavel stand by the fire, chatting with the policemen, stamping their feet. They both look really stressed. This is big. It's not like he's late home or something – they must think he's really run away.

"So, this morning. What do you remember?" The policewoman sits with her pen hovering over the page.

I take a deep breath. "It was like every morning

– Mum drove, I sat in the back. We went to my school first. I got out. Boom – that's it. What's happened to him?"

"Any more detail?" asks the policewoman, ignoring my question.

I wonder whether to tell her about the row and decide that it won't hurt. "Er, Noah tends to sit in the front seat – he's... Well, he does." I glance up at his mother sitting there working her way through a box of tissues. "Ever since he— Anyway, Mum suggested that we should both sit on the back seat, together, and Noah refused and in the confusion, he banged his nose..." I couldn't quite tell the whole truth. "And he gets nosebleeds really easily, so he bled over everything."

"Everything?"

"Er – my bag and his trousers. And the car. "

"I'll need your bag if you don't mind." She scribbles in her notebook. "So how would you say your relationship with Noah was?" The policewoman's voice seems very loud and everyone turns to look.

"Um," I say. "Stormy? No – distant."

She spends far too long writing "stormy", so I imagine she's also writing notes on how my face looks, my clothing, my eyebrows.

"Can I see your phone – you've had contact with him today?"

"Here," I say. "We were still in the car together when he sent that."

She reads the messages. Her eyes widen. "Let me get this clear, that was him talking to you." She points at the *I'll get you later* bit.

"Yup," I say. Over by the fire, the men stop talking and the room falls uncomfortably quiet.

Finally, when she seems to notice that everyone's listening, she takes a plastic bag from her pocket and slips my phone inside. "We'll just hang on to it for a bit – in case he contacts you. OK?"

Chapter 4

Another policewoman arrives to take Connor the gamekeeper off for questioning, and everyone looks embarrassed and shuffles their feet. Connor goes bright red. "I don't know a thing," he says to the room, but no one answers.

Dave blows his nose and pulls his collar up around his ears. I've never seen him look so human. I've always been a little scared of him. The sawmill's further out of the estate so he usually only comes in to help with the shoots. Everyone helps with the shoots. All winter, rich people come and shoot pheasants. Mostly they're pretty rubbish shots, but sometimes they're not and loads of dead birds fall in the woods and Connor's dogs pick them up and everyone eats pheasant for weeks. Sometimes, for real people, they shoot not real birds but clay birds instead. Clay pigeons. Then you just hear someone shout "Pull!" followed by two bangs and loads of shards of black pot fall all over the place. That's just noisy. I can see the fun in that – kind of like a big, real computer game. In the summer, very rich people come and fish. Not worm and bits of bacon fishing, but proper fly-fishing. Chris Mumford teaches them. They don't catch many, but we have a fishery on the estate full of baby trout that get put in the river from time to time. Sometimes there are too many fish, so they smoke them and we all eat smoked trout for ages.

I don't much like smoked trout. Or pheasant.

Lord B throws a log on the fire so violently that sparks burst up the chimney.

Lady B lets out a long sob.

I slip out through the front door.

Mum's not back when I let myself into the flat and listen out for Tai's tiny snores. Finding my bag, I empty it and take it to the policewoman in the main house.

"Thank you, Vivienne," she says, looking away, as if I'm dismissed. I want to ask again about Mum, but instead I return to our flat without a word, slamming our door behind me, shutting myself in.

This is my home, it's been my home for almost all my life, but it feels strange. Blue flickering lights from the police cars flash across the walls as if they're warning everyone out of their way, but there's no one to warn. Don't they ever turn them off?

I imagine the people in the house. Then there's me, here, and around us there's acres and acres of empty space, cut through by the river. They can't possibly have searched it all.

Tai wakes, pads over and lays his head on my foot.

"Hello, boy," I say, reaching to pick him up. Straight away he wriggles out of my arms and sniffs at the front door where he whines, scratching at the frame. He wants to go for a walk.

"I know, but I'm so hungry and..." I look out into the darkness – am I a little afraid? I'm never scared of the dark; that was Noah's thing. Not mine. But...

Kicking off my shoes, I rummage in the cupboard

for a packet of instant tomato soup.

"I'll make this really fast," I say, ripping off the top. I wait for the kettle to boil and watch the blue lights flicker through the blind.

I wish I knew more.

I wish I knew anything.

I wish Mum was here.

He hasn't come home, he wasn't there when Marion went to pick him up.

So he disappeared from school. Either someone has taken him – I dismiss that immediately. Or...

Teachers. Did he ever say anything about any teachers? At all?

Why did she ask that? Is Noah in love with his art teacher? Has he run away with someone? But I don't think anyone would fall in love with Noah. In fact, I can't think why anyone would want him at all. He's not cute, or charming, or funny or lovable. The only thing I can think is that he might have run away to make a protest.

That's almost possible. The last time we had a real talk – a proper conversation – was just before we left our junior schools. He told me his father wanted him to become a lawyer, like his uncle Peregrine, who's loaded. The idea was that he'd save the Blackwater Estate for future little Belcombes. Earn loads of money. He didn't mind the money bit, but he didn't want to have to do the studying. He wanted to be something else. Work with wood or maybe design things. He didn't really know, but he knew it wasn't a lawyer.

So perhaps this was just to upset his parents. Make them listen.

I think back to his mother weeping on the sofa. He's certainly achieved that – but then he's also upset my mum, or at least made her go off with the police, and all the staff at Blackwater are running around, and there are four police cars and a load of people in white scrabbling in the dark and the cold.

In fact, if he's sulking, he's making it everyone's business.

I pour the boiling water into a mug and add tomato-coloured sand. Stirring it into gloop I take it to the table and instinctively reach for my phone but it isn't there. The policewoman's got it. "This is bad, Tai," I say. "I'm cut off from the world."

Tai growls at the door. He lets out a little bark.

"Tai?"

Yapping again, he dances around the mat,

running back and forth.

"What's wrong?"

Unnerved, I approach the door sideways and peer through the window. Dave and Chris are out there chatting, halfway up the steps. They must hear me, or Tai, because a second later, Chris knocks on the door.

I let out a long breath. For some reason that made me really tense.

"Does that dog of yours need to go for a walk?" asks Chris, sounding super cheerful. "I thought you might be a bit nervous with all the commotion – don't know who's out here tonight. I could take him with me." He bites his lip. He definitely isn't as relaxed as his words and I wonder what it's like for all the estate workers – each one hauled off for questioning in turn.

Tai looks up at me, his tail wagging. "Thank you," I say.

"C'mon, lad – c'mon Tai." From the darkness, Dave lets out a little whistle. Tai stands in the doorway, looking up at me.

"Go on," I say. "They won't hurt."

Tai sniffs the air outside, and steps back.

"Here, lad." Chris crouches and gently strokes

Tai's head. Tai lets out a little sneeze, but he still won't go outside.

Dave leans forward and tries pulling at Tai's collar. Tai growls and Dave drops it as if it's hot. "Funny old dog," he says. Tai's never liked Dave. Nor have I. There is something formidable about him. Perhaps it's because he never says anything. He used to frown at us when we were little and we played around the sawmill. Mum said it was because it was a dangerous place to play. I reckoned it was because Dave doesn't like children.

"Oh, go on, Tai – please," I say.

But Tai won't move.

"Sorry, Chris, I don't really understand, but maybe he's spooked by all the blue lights. I think I'd better come too," I say, reaching for Mum's super-thick duffel coat and her wellies. At the last second I grab the set of keys that have a torch on them.

"S'pose so. If you don't mind doing a bit of looking about for the boy. We're still checking the estate." Chris leans forward and ruffles Tai's ears. "Daft dog."

"No, of course not," I say, jamming on a pair of gloves.

Dave wanders back down the steps. "Speak to

you later, mate," he says to Chris, and then, "Night, Viv."

I lock the door and follow Tai and Chris into the courtyard. Chris whistles and his dog, Lady, trots silently out of the shadows. Lady's a proper Border collie, a real sheepdog. She's trained and obedient. Tai is untrained and only does things for love. Or food. For a few minutes we walk in comfortable silence, Tai racing in circles around our legs, Lady keeping just out of the way of our feet. The police are still checking the Mini, while the front door of the house is open, and people are moving around inside. I can't see who though.

Chris opens the gate that leads into the gardens. "Keep our eyes open, eh?"

"Yes," I say, wondering whether I actually want to find Noah.

Our feet crunch from gravel to frozen grass.

Above us the first stars twinkle. It's ferociously cold. So cold that my ears hurt even under my hood. I look up at the black shape of Chris next to me. He's massive, almost twice my height, and very reassuring. All my life he's been the bear of the estate – large and safe and reliable – although Mum's always said, "Still waters run deep" and tapped her nose. I heard a rumour that he might once have been a pub fighter, but that could just be estate talk.

He's always been a part of my life. Just like the river he looks after, I suppose. A presence.

A long flapping sound begins on the water and a slow *whoop, whoop* as a bird takes off.

"Swan?" I ask as the wings creak over our heads.

"Yup," he says.

We walk on a little further. Woodsmoke drifts across us from one of the cottages, sweet and kippery. "You'd never seen a swan," starts Chris, "when you came here. Remember the day you and your ma arrived – fresh off the plane from Singapore?" I can hear the smile in his voice. "Swan, swan, swan! You chased them everywhere – right into the river. Fearless, you were."

"Did you rescue me from the river?"

"Both of you in the end. You and the boy."

"We got on then, I think," I say, trying to sift through the memories to a time when Noah and I actually might have been friends.

"Mebbe."

We swing around the corner of the sheds. "Though it seems only a second later that I came across you two fighting like proper boxers."

It must have been four years later. We were about six. Not for the first time, Noah had pushed me into the river and then blamed me for playing near the bank. Like it was my idea, and he'd heroically hauled me out instead of what he actually did, which was to run off and laugh up a tree as I struggled not to drown. I'd gone for him, kicking and punching. "You gave me some of your soup from your thermos because I got so told off by Lady B I didn't want to go home."

"Ha," Chris laughs. "Never seen a girl fight like you. Dead handy with that fist." He stops and sniffs the air. "If I hadn't pulled you off, you would've seriously hurt him."

I take it as a compliment and smile to myself.

As we pass the tall yew trees that mark the entrance to the gardens, he grabs my shoulder. "Shh, hear that?" he asks.

I stop and listen. I can't hear anything. I peer into the darkness, imagining faces in the foliage.

I don't come in here much any more, but I used to wander in with some of the other children from the estate. There was a girl called Daisy with a younger brother and sister, Seb and Molly, but they moved away when their parents got another gardening job in Wales. We played here but mostly we messed about in the shallows, searching the bottom for treasures. Bottles, buckles, coins. Paddling in the ice-cold clear water over the squidgy gravel bottom, crayfish and tiny minnows brushing our feet. Sometimes we swam and it was so cold I could hardly breathe, and on hot days we might jump from the bridge into the deepest part of the river and run out screaming from the cold. Noah didn't join in much. Perhaps he wasn't allowed to.

I shiver. It's not the weather to think about cold water.

"Did you hear anything?" he asks me.

"Nope," I answer.

"Must have been a rabbit," he says, and we walk on and I feel the tension in the air. It's as if he's expecting to find something – Noah? A stranger?

The hairs on the back of my neck prickle and I shake my head. Next to me Tai stops, sniffs and shivers.

"Someone walked over your grave, dog?" mutters Chris.

One star shines low in the sky in the band of almost-green almost-blue that throws the chimneys of the house into silhouette. Leafless trees hang overhead as we make our way around past the greenhouse to the orchard. I try to stick to the path, but my hood catches in the branches so I have to walk through the fallen apples left out for the blackbirds in the long grass.

"Mind out for the squishy ones," says Chris.

I don't manage to avoid them. Some are crunchy, but others are soft, my foot releasing a quick smell of cider and vomit. Over to our right two torches flash in the hedge. That'll be Shona and Tony, the gardeners.

"All right?" Chris calls to them. "Found anything?"

"Not a peep," Tony calls back. "Give it till midnight."

"Such an idiot," I say under my breath.

"Wha's that?" says Chris.

"Noah – I just think – oh – why would Noah run away tonight – when it's so cold? He's stupid. It's just attention seeking."

"Not for me to say, but he's not the brightest button in the box," says Chris, ducking under a branch. "Perhaps he's gone to a friend's house – forgot to tell anyone."

"I don't think he's got any friends."
"Ah," says Chris.
"All this fuss – police and everything. And Mum," I say, feeling crosser and crosser. "You know, when we find him, I'm going to kill him. I don't know why I didn't do it earlier."
Chris says nothing.
"Thing is – all the disruption, he's got no idea of what he's done. When he comes back, when he's made his silly little point, he'll think everything's normal. But it won't be because my lovely mum's spent all evening being questioned by the police and being suspected. It's not fair – I'll hit him again."
"Thump him once today, did you?" asks Chris, sounding amused.
"Er – well, not really a thump..." I backtrack. "I kind of gave him a nosebleed."
"Ah – that's why they're all over the car then." We walk on. "Did you tell them that?"
"Yeah, but I think they think I did it on purpose – or that Mum stabbed him or something."
"Oh, I don't expect they think that. They're questioning us all, you know. Lord B took a hell of a grilling."

"So it's not just Mum."

"No – it's not just your mum."

We swing round to walk the other side of the orchard. "Do you know when he disappeared?"

"Mid-afternoon," says Chris. "But everything's rumour, you know how this place is. The police don't tell us nothing."

In his pocket, Chris's phone rings and I listen as he talks to someone at the other end.

"Yes, yes."

The rectangle of yellow shines on to his grey stubbly cheek and I drift off as he swings around, with his back to me, talking and listening.

"I'm walking with young Vivienne as it happens."

Beneath my feet the grass rustles, the splinters of ice falling around my boots, the ground hard, like iron. Inside the boots, my feet are freezing too. Tights just aren't enough to keep this kind of cold out and this is far too cold for a person to sleep under a hedge. Noah must have found somewhere under cover, but where would he go? Why would he do it? Why would he keep it going so long?

You fool, Noah. But this time I don't say it out loud.

"The dump – over by Pond's End – yes, sir, if

you say so."

I scour the landscape in my head.

Woods.

Dens.

Farm.

As the tiny streak of sky turns totally dark, I remember the dump. It's forbidden. Well, at least it always was. It used to be a collection of farm machinery surrounded by random pieces of rusting metal, barbed wire and stuff left over from before the Second World War.

"I'll go together with Vivienne. Sharp eyes and that."

He listens.

"Uh-huh. OK, we'll take a look then. I got a torch."

The phone goes dark. "Come on, Viv – let's see if he's hiding down there."

At the end of the orchard is a gate that lets us out into a small field. With cold fingers I struggle with the loop of baler twine that holds it shut. Chris reaches over my shoulder and opens it easily. While he closes it, I stop and listen.

A screech owl.

A fox.

Maybe a distant pheasant, and all around us the cold falls, a vertical icy wind heading for the earth.

Orion shines overhead.

We don't need to speak, we both know the way, and we walk on, the dogs snuffling and dancing around our legs. Tai seems happy with Lady, even if he wouldn't go on his own with Chris.

Frozen tussocks catch on my wellies, and we stomp across the field, heading towards the river. A little way to our left, a two-plank weed rack crosses the narrowest part of the stream. There's wire netting over the wood, so it shouldn't be too slippery, and a thin hand rail, but I take it carefully. I don't want to fall in, not because I'd drown, but because it would be just another thing to make me even angrier with Noah.

The other bank is boggy and not yet frozen and we pick our way through two strands of barbed wire rather than walking all the way along to the stile, but my coat snags on the lower strand. Fiddling about in the dark, with my tiny key torch lighting up one finger at a time, I curse Noah until I manage to free myself and follow Chris over the next field towards a distant clump of woodland. Sheep rustle in the dark, looming towards us and then trotting away. Chris whistles to Lady, who pads obediently alongside him. I have to hang on to Tai's collar to stop him chasing after the sheep.

"Hello, sheep," I say, aware of their smell of warm wool and poo. There's a slight crunch with each step, and the cold begins to eat into my lower jaw. *Noah, I am so going to kill you when I find you.*

As we reach the brow of the field, we're met by another fence. I pull the wires apart and lift my foot into the gap.

"No need for that," says Chris, and he lifts me like a small child straight over the top, while he hurdles the wires as if they weren't there.

"Oh," I say, landing back in the grass. Ahead of us, the little group of trees seems bigger, darker, and I keep stomping towards it, telling myself that there's nothing at all spooky about it – even though, when we were six, we named it Dead Things Wood, because we'd found a dead rabbit and then a dead fox hanging on the barbed wire, like someone had put them there. And besides, Chris is very near. I can't see him, but I can hear him.

The trees loom over us, the bare branches of ashes and beeches cupped against the sky. Cutting it out, holding me in.

"Torch time," says Chris, startling me, and the pool of bright light makes the black around us even blacker. "I'll check right down the far end – there's a shed I keep some tools in. Wait here and I'll be back. Don't move."

The light of the torch bounces off metal and hedgerow, and fades as Chris vanishes up to the left. I don't really remember a shed, but I do remember a car. A black, mossy car.

The more I stare into the dark, the surer I am that I can make out its shape. Carefully, I pick my way into the trees until the muddled mass of forgotten farm machinery reveals itself behind the ring of trunks. In the distance I can see Chris's torchlight bouncing off the undergrowth, illuminating patches of green and spots of brown. Straining my eyes in the darkness, I stop at the edge and look down. It's not a cliff so much as a steep chalky slope and I know that at the bottom is the old car with one headlight and no wheels. I shine my pathetic torch down the slope until it catches on something metal. Then something glass.

Yes.

The beam reflects from the windscreen, which is scratched but intact, and I wobble it over the doors, swinging it back and forth so that I can see if anyone responds.

There's no sign of life but I slither down the slope, catching my hand on a bramble and sliding part of the way on my bum.

The car sits heavily in the middle of everything else. Doors closed.

"Come on, Viv," I say, and grab the driver's door, yanking it open and standing back. From a couple of paces away I shine the light on to the inside. Bindweed has grown through from the back seat and now trails undisturbed across the steering wheel.

Frost falls through a rusted hole in the roof.

There's no one there, and no one's been there for a while.

"Damn you, Noah Belcombe. Where the hell are you?!" I shout to the stars, and run for Chris.

Chapter 5

Mum's there when I get back and she leaps to the door.

"Where have you been?" she says, grabbing the coat off my back and kneeling down to help me with my boots.

"I went out with Chris, took Tai for a walk, and we were looking for Noah, like everyone else," I say, wriggling out of Mum's coat. "Where were you?"

I pull at my tights. There's a big hole in the toe.

Mum sits back and I see that she's white and red and streaky like someone who's been in tears for hours.

"I've –" She flaps her hand. "S'OK," she mutters.

"What?" I say. She's not telling me something. "Where did you go? When did all this happen?"

"Half past four?" she says. "I went to pick him up and – he didn't come out of school." She's staring at her hands as if the story's written there. "It took until ages later for the school to be sure he really wasn't there – and then I went into the headmaster's office and he rang the Belcombes, and the police because – Well, he rang the police."

"So why are they searching here?"

"Someone said they saw him catch the bus out of town – or they saw someone in a St David's uniform catch the bus. I think that's what the police think..."

"They took my phone, and my bag," I say.

"Oh, no," she replies. "That seems unnecessary."

"They don't think I've got..."

"I don't know what they think."

She picks at the skin next to her thumbnail, pulling off a tiny shred.

"Mum," I say, pointing. "Don't."

She smiles at me and sits on her hands. "Thing is," she says in the end. And then she stops again, swallowing and nodding her head as she speaks, as if she's explaining it to herself as much as me. "The police." She pauses. "The police seem to think I might have somehow done something with him." She looks up, her lip wobbling. She gulps air, and stifles a sob, but the words that follow are barely even a whisper. "It's the blood in the car. I told them that it happened this morning…" She stops and wipes the heels of her palms over her eyes. "But I'm not sure they believe me. That's why they've taken your bag – it's the blood, Viv. The stupid blood."

"Oh, Mum," I say, squeezing on to the sofa alongside her and linking my arm through hers. "But there wasn't very much of it. And it was on my bag too – and I told them I'd had a bit of a – you know, scrap, with him. They surely don't think you've got anything to do with this. It's Noah being an idiot. It must be. He's trying to teach his parents a lesson, surely."

"Hmmm." Mum blows her nose and fiddles with the skin on the edge of her nail again. Her fingers are raw. She looks to one side. "Do you remember Sanjeev?"

"Yes," I say. "He was lovely. You went out bowling with him, didn't you?"

Mum nods. "It got complicated. He had a child, and there was you, and babysitting, and I – probably wasn't really ready." A shadow of sadness settles over her blotchy face.

"What about him?" I ask.

"Well, he's disappeared too. He didn't turn up to collect his daughter from school."

"I don't understand."

"He's Noah's rugby teacher – the coach of the team. He didn't finish the day at St David's, and now he's missing too."

"And you think they think you're working together? That you've both kidnapped Noah?" I look at Mum. She nods.

"But they can't think that, surely. You haven't seen him for years, have you? And he's a nice guy – he'd never do anything stupid like that. He doesn't need the money, does he?"

Mum sighs. "Probably he doesn't. And you're right, Sanjeev is a lovely man. I do hope you're right, that Noah's run off and hidden somewhere. But his mum, poor Julia, she's completely devastated by it. She's in bits."

Between the slats of the blind I peer out into the courtyard. The police cars are still there, but their lights have stopped flashing. The front door opens and I see Chris Mumford come down the steps and clamber into his Land Rover. His walk is heavy, his face exhausted. The door to the house closes and I can only imagine what is going on inside.

* * *

Later, I lie in the dark listening to leaves falling from the beech trees outside, and wondering.

If this is Noah's idea of a joke, then he's stringing it out. I really thought he might have gone to hide in the car. And then got scared when darkness crept into the quarry. And got stuck. And I kind of imagined myself rescuing him and telling him not to be so stupid and bringing him home to his parents and being hailed a bit of a hero.

That's sort of how I imagined it. But he wasn't there.

My dream-me runs around the entire estate, the village and even Alchester itself trying to find his hiding place.

Eventually, I fall asleep.

* * *

Banging wakes me. It's our front door but Mum's there before me. Tai is dancing around her feet, yapping.

It's completely dark outside and a strange policewoman steps into our hallway. She doesn't seem to notice me and fixes on Mum. I glance at the oven clock: it's six fifteen. Middle of the night.

"Mrs Lin, would you come in to answer a few questions, please? And make a statement."

"Now?" says Mum, pulling her dressing gown cord tight around her middle.

"If you wouldn't mind. There's been a development," says the policewoman.

"What?" says Mum. "Have you found him?"

The policewoman says nothing but stands in the open doorway letting the wind and leaves in and the warmth out.

"What about Viv? How will she get to school?" says Mum.

"She'll be fine. Lady Belcombe says she can stay in the house."

* * *

I watch Mum leave. She waves from the back of the police car and shortly afterwards I perch on one of the dead cow sofas in Blackwater House, wearing my school uniform at six thirty in the morning. Lady Belcombe stands next to me, tears streaming down her face, and I feel awkward. Almost more awkward than I've ever felt. If she was Mum, I'd give her a hug, but she isn't. She's just a woman we've lived next door to for practically my entire life.

And she may be missing her son, but I'm missing my mum.

She nibbles at a nail and checks and rechecks her phone. Her anxiety is almost another person in the room. This must be driving her mad, not knowing. Lady B always knows everything.

As if she's suddenly noticed me, she blows her nose and disappears upstairs, which leaves me, the slumbering fire and a slumbering policewoman.

I wish I knew what had happened. I wish I had my phone.

I wish I had Tai, but the police have handed him over to Tony the gardener.

Poor Tai.

Poor Tony.

I try to hide inside one of the enormous leather armchairs, pulling my legs up and curling them between the arms.

Unaware of me, Lord Belcombe stomps through the hall dressed in a mix of pyjamas and tweeds, talking to someone on his phone.

"Peregrine, I'm terrified. I'm absolutely terrified. What if something *has* happened..." He stops, apparently addressing the corner of the room.

"Yes, yes – no – nothing like that." There's a pause.

"We've had no kind of demand, you understand. But if we did – you would help – wouldn't you? We've asked Julia's cousin, but I think he's a bit strapped for cash and we're completely skint."

His voice is so clipped that even when he whispers I can understand every syllable.

"No, as I say, no one's actually asked ... and it might not be that. It could be some awful—" His voice breaks. "Some ghastly accident. He could be lying somewhere..."

He turns, his face wet with tears, sees me, and thunders off up the stairs.

Listening to his retreating footsteps, I curl tighter on the armchair, pulling a cushion under my ear and grabbing another to hug. I close my eyes but I become aware of a shuffling presence. Opening one eye very slightly I see Maria, the Filipino woman who cooks for the Belcombes. She's wearing a pink padded dressing gown and silver fluffy slippers and she's holding out a little tray with two mugs overflowing with cream and marshmallows.

"Here, Vivienne." She places the tray on a small table and sits down next to me. "I thought you might like this, and I can keep you company before you go to school."

"Oh, Maria." I wriggle myself around in the chair. "Thank you." I take a mug from her and hold it up to my mouth. It's scalding.

We sit with Tigger, the cat, listening to the wind, the crackle of the fire and the house creaking above our heads. She blows on her hot drink. I blow on mine.

I've spent lots of time drinking Maria's hot chocolate, but always in the kitchen, never out here in the hall, and I can't work out how to behave. Am I here as a neighbour in distress? Or the nanny's daughter? Or the daughter of the prime suspect?

Glancing over to the policewoman, I see that she's barely awake. I nudge Maria and whisper, "When they took Mum they said there had been a development."

Maria nods and stares into the fire.

"Do you know what...?"

She puts her finger to her lips but murmurs, "They've found his phone."

My jaw drops. "What?"

Maria nods. "Yes," she hisses. "Nowhere near his school or here, apparently."

"He wouldn't hide without it, would he?"

"Not on purpose, I wouldn't think. So they're going to move the search elsewhere."

"I suppose he might have dropped it in the dark," I say.

Maria tilts her head from side to side. "He might," she says.

Wow.

Once again I reach for my phone, which isn't there. I really want to talk to Mum about this.

"But they don't really think Mum's got anything to do with it, do they?"

Maria shrugs. "Are you going to be all right without her?" she says, her eyes wide over her mug.

For a second I wonder what she means. All right for today? All right forever? "What? She won't be gone for long – will she?" I say, struggling to speak.

"I hope not," says Maria. She puts down her mug and leans forward to put another log on the fire. "I very much hope not." And we sit there in silence listening to the storm beginning outside.

Chapter 6

Sharon, Chris's girlfriend, drives me to school.

I get to sit in the front but I have to move a huge pile of holiday brochures on to the back seat in order to get in. "Sorry, Viv, just dreaming!" she says, flinging the last ones over her shoulder. Earlier, I told them I could take the bus, but Sharon rang the house and insisted. "Honestly – it's so easy, I'm just next door and Chris has already started work out on the river." I don't really know her, I've just seen her out with Chris and I know they live together on the other side of the stable block. She's friendly and is obviously trying to be really normal, which means that she talks too much.

"So, Viv, where would you normally be dropped – right outside the school gates? I know I couldn't stand that, soooo embarrassing. I used to make my mum drop me streets away so that no one could see – and what about dinner – do you need dinner money cos I'm sure I've got a few pound coins in my purse—"

"I'm fine, thanks," I say.

She babbles and I drift. I'm thinking about Mum in the police station. Making a statement...

"Does 'making a statement' to the police mean the same as being arrested?"

"Thinking about your mum?" Sharon clunks the gears. She's a terrible driver although to be fair it's a terrible old car. "No, I think it's like – helping with their enquiries? You know – you hear that a lot on the news. No, they can't think she's got anything to do with his disappearance. Don't worry about it. She'll be back soon." She swings round a corner, narrowly missing a cyclist. "They've taken Dave too, you know – not that he knows anything, bless him, wouldn't hurt a fly, but I think they're really concentrating on this Sanjeev guy. He's gotta be the one – if it's a kidnapping, that is."

She shudders to a halt at the bus stop opposite the school. I'm really early, but I don't want to make her wait so I start to open the door. She puts her hand on my sleeve. "Really – don't worry about your mum, love. She'll be back later on... If she's not, I'll make sure someone comes to pick you up – so you don't have to make your way back on the bus, just in case – you know."

I run into school. It's still raining. It hasn't stopped since six o'clock this morning and there's a huge puddle forming outside the library block. I forgot my coat. Idiot.

The only person there is Ciara. She gets dropped off early. I honestly don't know her, but it feels rude to sit on the other side of the room so I sit down nearby and reach for the newspaper that's folded on the coffee table.

"Read the one about the plane," she says. "It's, like, sooooo unlikely." She pulls her phone out of her bag and begins to text.

"I will," I say, flicking through the first few pages and noting that there is absolutely nothing about Noah.

Perhaps it's a secret. Perhaps they don't want anyone to know.

I read the article about a woman who had to land a plane because the pilot passed out.

Like that ever happened. I'm just getting to the possible bit, where they got married afterwards, when a girl and a boy I don't know swoop up behind Ciara and push her and her wheelchair off down the corridor.

"Bye," shouts Ciara over her shoulder.

"Bye," I call back down the corridor.

"There you are!" yells Sabriya across the lobby. "We've been waiting for you at the bus stop. Why didn't you answer our texts?"

"Sorry," I say.

"You a prospective parent or what?" says Joe behind her. "Reading the paper and that. Ooooh, look at her – posh house, posh paper."

"Shut up, Joe. Guess what?" I say.

"What?" they ask.

"I—" And suddenly I'm filled with doubt. I don't know if I'm allowed to know – to say – if it's not in the paper. "Noah's disappeared," I hiss.

"The toad baby?" asks Joe.

"Yeah."

"Why would you run away from all that?" asks Sabriya. "I reckon he's been kidnapped."

And the bell rings.

* * *

"And so the infinitive, *dormir* – what does that mean, Harry Pole?" Mr Roberts shouts across the classroom where Harry Pole is slumped over his desk with his head on his arms.

"It means sleep, sir," shouts Melody Pippin, possibly the most annoying person in the school.

"*To* sleep, Melody, to sleep. Now…"

I drift off, staring out of the window at the sports fields of Herschel High and, in the distance, the tower of the chapel at St David's. Moving my chair about a millimetre forward, I can see past our sports hall right over to the St David's main building. It's like they built Herschel High in the aura of St David's – as if it would rub off and improve the place.

"And how about *être*? Vivienne?"

I flush hot and cold and blurt, "To see?"

Some of the class laugh – they're the people who've done French before – but I know that most of us are clueless. "To be," mutters Nadine, next to me.

"To be?" I repeat.

"Yes, Vivienne. Very good, Nadine."

Kanye McAllister pokes me in the back. I ignore him.

I fall back to staring out of the window, but this time my view's blocked by a police car parked right in front of the main building at St David's. So they're searching the last place he was seen. Which makes sense.

Twirling my pen between my fingers I try to work out what could possibly have happened to him.

Kidnap? But there must be nicer people to kidnap and I know that the Belcombes own half of the county but they don't actually have any money. Everyone knows that. Or everyone should since that article that Lady B wrote about "make do and mend" and the trials of landowning without any cash. They keep stuff shiny on the surface for the summer visitors, the fishermen and the people who come to shoot, but underneath it's pretty crumbly.

Perhaps he owes someone money.

Perhaps he's been messing about on the dark web and brought a gang of criminals down on his head, not so much a kidnap as someone seizing him to punish him.

Perhaps his dad's been messing about on the dark web and brought a gang of criminals down on his head – and they've seized Noah to punish Lord B.

The idea immediately sounds ridiculous.

Which means he must have run away. Without his phone – so no one could trace him. Just so that he didn't have to be a lawyer.

"Wow," I say out loud and everyone stares. "Sorry," I say, and Nadine crumbles into a heap of giggles.

* * *

The rain has become a fixture. It won't stop, and no one comes to pick me up. I get soaked on my way back, struggling up the driveway against the swirling leaves, walking through the afternoon gloom into the courtyard. I've got my key ready but at the top of the steps I find a policeman in white overalls examining the wellies I wore last night.

"Hey—" I say.

"Sarge," he shouts into the room, and another policeman in white appears in the hall.

"What's happening?" I say.

"We've got a warrant to search this flat. Do you live here?"

"I do," I say, hearing the wobble in my voice.

"Vivienne Lin," he says.

I nod. I don't trust myself to speak.

"I think you'd better go over to the house. I'm fairly sure they've made arrangements for you to sleep there."

"Sleep? What about Mum?"

"She ... probably won't be back tonight. I think you'll be fine in the house. Food and that," he says vaguely. "Stella – how are you getting on with the bathroom?" He turns away from me as if I don't matter.

I stand and stare for a moment, and then, realising that it's making me feel worse, turn back across the courtyard. The main door is closed so I go up the steps and ring the bell.

Lady B opens it. "Oh," she says, disappointed. "It's you."

"They're searching our flat," I say, clamping my nail to my palm, so that I don't cry. "I don't have anywhere to go."

She waves me past, back to the leather sofas, the fire, the crackling silence.

On the edge of tears, I clutch Tigger and watch the darkness fall. The torches of searching police people come on across the garden and the sergeant lets me into the flat to get pyjamas, clothes and a toothbrush. The men in white overalls squeeze back as I come into the flat and I imagine them going through everything, including my room. All my clothes. All my underclothes – clean and dirty.

Oh, no.

I'm still cringing when Lady B's phone rings. Her fingers dance across the screen and she walks to the window. "Yes – Julia Belcombe here."

She listens.

"Oh, for goodness' sake, don't bother me with this now. Can't you just put it somewhere cold? It's nearly winter – everywhere's cold."

She listens again.

"Use a car. Use anything."

She listens again.

"Biscuits – get biscuits. I don't know, bourbons, custard creams. He likes both. Now, get off my phone."

"Honestly," she sighs. "Some people have no sense of a situation." She slips the phone back into her pocket and straightens her skirt. She turns to me and almost smiles. But I can see she's only just holding it all together.

"Vivienne, you can sleep in the box room," she says. "It's cosy. And Maria will give you supper in the kitchen."

And that's it.

Chapter 7

Maria and I watch a film with Bruce Willis and eat pasta in a revolting thick creamy sauce. Of course, I grew up running around this kitchen, but it feels empty with just the two of us. No Mum, no Noah. I notice how high the ceiling is, the tiled white walls. The cavernous fireplace guarded by ironwork that must have once roasted a lamb. Everything echoes and the tiny telly perched on the end of the table seems brash in this ancient place.

Maria must be used to it. She chatters from time to time, reads a romance novel and, quite suddenly in the middle of the film, starts making a Skype call in a language I don't understand, laughing and chatting with her daughter back home in the Philippines.

I pull my dressing gown tighter and wait for the film to finish.

At nine o' clock I wave goodbye to Maria, who's still talking to her relatives, and creep up the back stairs to my bedroom. It's tiny. But Lady B's right; compared to the rest of the house, it's cosy. Maria has put an ancient pink electric blanket in my bed and although I unplug it in case it explodes overnight, the bed's toasty.

I sit with the curtains open, watching the rain beat against the windows. I wonder if Tai's doing the same round at Tony's house. I'll try and get him back tomorrow. Surely no one would mind him sleeping up here with me, would they? I do miss him.

I check out the little bookshelf. Beatrix Potter, Rudyard Kipling, *The Water Babies*. There's nothing published in the last one hundred years. I reread *Mrs Tiggywinkle*, then look at a book called *Johnny Crow's Garden*. Weird. For a while I sit and hug my knees and watch torches wandering around the grounds.

I wish I had my phone.

I wish I'd brought something modern to read.

I wish Mum was here.

I also kind of wish that Noah wasn't lost.

Just a tiny bit.

About a millimetre.

Needing a wee is what finally forces me out of bed. The landing's deserted and I tiptoe down to the bathroom, which is huge and empty and has the Belcombe crest all over the porcelain. Pulling the chain on the toilet I set off a load of scary plumbing noises that thunder through the pipes, so I sneak back towards my room hoping that no one's going to come and find out what's going on.

Pausing on the landing, I listen to try and work out where everyone is. Below my feet a television rumbles, and then off to the left there are male voices. The police? In the hall?

Distantly, someone's playing a piano – that's probably Lady B. She used to play incidental music for all of us children when we made little movies and showed them back to her and Mum. Just now, it sounds very mournful, like a siren song – calling to someone.

The floorboards creak as I make my way along the landing to my room. On the way, I pass Noah's bedroom. I'm kind of surprised it's not covered in police tape so I push the door open and peek in. A little light comes with me from the landing, but I turn the main light on and decide that if anyone asks, I can just say I'm looking for something to read.

He has a bookshelf full of shiny new books. Some of them look really dull. *Law in a Modern Age.* What? *Constitutional Reforms and the House of Lords*? Seriously?

On the shelf below, I find some untouched fiction and help myself to a small stack.

I put the books on the bed and look around the rest of the room. It's a weird mixture of boy and man. A Star Wars dressing gown hangs on the back of the door. He must have grown out of that by now. Some very expensive headphones dangle from the door handle, and there's a thousand-pound computer gleaming on the desk. A Lego dinosaur's working as a bookend on the law shelf; there are three soft rabbits on the bed. I recognise one of them as Herbert. Herbert travelled with Noah everywhere. I remember Noah standing, holding

Herbert and watching Daisy and me building a den. I can see now that he wanted to join in, but at the time he just looked as if he wanted to destroy it. Which to be fair is exactly what he'd done to our last den. I pick Herbert up and give him a hug and arrange him on the pillow. I'd take him to keep me company if that wasn't too much of a liberty.

And I'm surprised that if Noah's on the run he didn't take Herbert.

Perhaps he didn't have time.

Presumably the police have checked his computer but I switch it on anyway. It asks me for a password and I look up at the top of the screen – there's a Post-it note – "TheEmpireStrikesBack". So I type it in and the computer pings into action. He's got a really lame screensaver of some weird gaming hulk striding through a destroyed city. I noodle through his emails – all of them spam – and then check out everything else.

I work my way through a series of icons. There are three flight simulation games and a stack of gaming sites I've never heard of. Maybe my theory of him owing money to some distant criminal ring is spot on. Maybe he's really annoyed someone in a way that I don't understand. As I look through his browsing history most of it is incomprehensible to me and I wonder at the loneliness of someone who spends their life talking to unreal people on the other side of the world about imaginary creatures.

"Hmm, Noah," I say out loud. "You're very sad."

I keep clicking and then find he's got a couple of social media pages, hardly any friends – but no recent posts.

I sigh, long and hard, and close down all the things I've opened up, only I'm a bit slow and I'm not really concentrating and before I've actually switched the wretched thing off, a policewoman's standing behind me with her arms crossed, and her face even crosser.

* * *

"So what exactly *were* you doing?" the policewoman asks me again.

"I was bored, I went into Noah's room to borrow some books and then I just … saw the computer and wondered if there might be anything to say – you know – where he'd gone. I didn't mean to … upset anyone."

It sounds pathetic, very pathetic.

Lord B is sitting on the arm of an armchair and

staring at me. Normally a restrained man, I can see he's furious, and I feel terrible. He stands up and begins to pace the room.

The policewoman starts to talk. "And how did—"

But Lord B waves his hand at her and cuts in. "Did it not occur to you that you were staying in our house, on our hospitality?" He doesn't exactly shout so much as hiss. "That, despite our son's disappearance, we were extending the hand of friendship? We were putting ourselves out when we were at our lowest ebb. Eh?" He turns to glare at me. "We gave you a room, a bed, food, warmth, succour. We fed you. We cared for you." He turns away again. "And, and – and that this, this abuse of us, was a gross – rank – appalling way to treat us? Did it never occur to you that you were behaving like a churl – a person with not a jot of morality? Eh? Did it not cross your tiny mind that you should never have poked around outside the room that we gave you? That you should have had the decency to keep yourself to yourself. And, most monstrously, had you never thought that when you clicked on Facebook, or whatever it was, that it would trigger the little light that gave us a moment's blissful hope? That for a second, we thought Noah was accessing his page from somewhere – that he was safe? Did that not occur to you, Vivienne? Hmmm?" Swinging round he faces me again, his eyes, tear-filled and angry, burn at me.

"I—"

But he hasn't finished. "Can you imagine how awful it is to lose a child? To conjure images of your child alone and scared in a cold landscape – possibly lost, possibly distraught – running. Eh? Fear? My fear, his fear – and then you fed it with hope? Or are you just utterly, utterly, stupid?"

He stomps out of the room and slams the door.

I let out my breath. Even the policewoman lets out a long sigh. She blinks and looks back at her notebook.

I glance from her to the floor and back to her.

"But…?"

"Right, Vivienne. Back to bed, and stay there please. OK?"

"He's not – that's not." I can't say anything coherent. "I didn't do it on purpose – doesn't he…?"

The policewoman looks up at me and I have to look away. Tears of utter fury force their way down my cheeks, so many that they drip from my chin. I'm embarrassed and I don't think anyone has ever been that angry with me. Not even Mum, not ever.

"Viv?" asks the policewoman.

"Can I have my phone back?" I mutter eventually.

"Oh, I didn't realise we had it. I'll put in a request. Off you go now." She smiles kindly at me, which makes me want to cry even more. "Wash your face – you'll feel better."

But before I leave, the landline rings.

Lord B comes back into the room. Under his mane of grey curly hair his face is blotchy, and Lady B appears from somewhere, her hair a mess, followed by a policeman.

They all stare at the bleating handset. The policeman plugs an earphone into his ear and nods at Lord B.

"Hello? Geoffrey Belcombe here," he says slowly.

There's a pause.

"Oh?"

"Yes."

"Yes, I do."

"Can I speak to him?" he says very quickly. "Please – please – oh!"

And he lets the receiver fall from his ear.

"He's been kidnapped." He turns to his wife, sobs breaking up his words. "That was the kidnappers. They're going to send us a photo as proof."

Chapter 8

"That," says Nadine at school the next day, "is the most exciting thing that's ever happened here. Isn't it?"

Joe shakes his head. "Yup – a person of our own age, being held against their will by a PE teacher. As good as it gets."

"Shut up, Joe. You know what I mean."

"And it's him – the most loathsome person we know," says Sabriya. "I mean, it's sort of karma, isn't it?"

"Suppose so," I say.

Ever since last night I've felt completely dreamlike.

I don't think I slept. The porridge tasted like wallpaper paste, the orange juice was just sharp. Maria's words went over my head.

Seeing Lord B so angry and then the phone call, it suddenly feels as if someone's died – and I haven't got Mum and it feels as if she's died too. I loathe Noah. "But I've known him all my life."

"Ooooh – best friends now, are we? Gonna sell the story to the newspapers?" asks Joe.

"Shut up, Joe," says Sabriya.

"I get you," says Nadine. "But . . . it's still exciting. Isn't it?"

We stand shivering under the eaves at the back of the gym. My shoes are damp, my feet are cold. Nadine's wearing the scratchy school sweater under her jacket and even she's shuddering. "And I'm worried about Mum. She's been with the police for more than twenty-four hours. They've taken her for their enquiries. They took her at six o' clock yesterday morning. They think she's in league with Sanjeev Gupta, the missing PE teacher."

"Is taking someone away at that hour in the morning even legal?" asks Sabriya.

"Yeah," says Joe, knowingly. "They do drug raids in the middle of the night. If they think it's a crime like murder they can hold someone for thirty-six hours."

We all look at Joe and he reddens. "Yeah, well, I've seen it on telly."

"Murder? Who said anything about murder?" I say.

"Maybe kidnap is just as awful in the eyes of the law," says Nadine.

"I don't expect they think she did it. I mean, you'd know, wouldn't you?" says Sabriya, pulling her jacket right across her chest and jamming her hands in her opposite pockets. "Wouldn't you?"

* * *

All morning I think about it.

Would I know?

I'd know if Mum had hidden Noah in the wardrobe. Or locked him in our ancient car or somewhere. But then, so would the forensic people.

For the thousandth time I reach for my phone, which isn't there.

And then I start to feel angry.

Angry with the police for taking Mum away in the dark of the early morning.

Angry with Noah for being kidnapped.

Angry with Sanjeev for having a relationship

with Mum and disappearing at the same time as Noah.

Angry with St David's for being rubbish at keeping their students safe.

Angry with the Belcombes for being so, so, so much better than we are.

Angry with Lord Belcombe for being angry with me.

Angry with the kidnappers for exploding my life, for all of it.

I look up at Miss Foulkes, who's trying to persuade Jimmy Speckles to sit down, and I feel angry with her too – for being so incompetent – and Jimmy Speckles for being disruptive and I stand up and walk out of the class.

I go hot and cold but I keep walking.

"Vivienne. Vivienne! Where do you think—" And the door swings shut behind me and I'm in the corridor kind of uncertain about where to go, which way to go, how to go home, because go home I must because I have to know what's going on.

* * *

Señora Delgado comes out to talk to me by the fence at the edge of the hockey pitch, and I explain. Handing me a tissue she suggests she rings the

Belcombes from her mobile.

"What is the number, Vivienne?"

Personally, I think that's quite brave of her – bearing in mind they're in the middle of a kidnap situation, and all the stuff that Lord B said last night, and how Lady B responded to the conversation about biscuits – but Señora Delgado is calm and nice and smiley and makes me feel a little bit better, and a little bit guiltier about being so histrionic.

"It must be very hard for Lady Belcombe," she says when she puts the phone back in her pocket. "Losing your child. Living there in the middle of the countryside," she shudders. "With no … sophisticated company. So isolated."

"Not that isolated – we're only a few miles out of town and there are loads of people on the estate."

"Hmmm." Señora Delgado stares into the distance. "But no one is from her world. She was such an important figure in journalism. She used to work undercover, you know; investigate. She gave it all up to marry Lord Belcombe – who is, I must say, very charming. But still, she must miss that excitement, that acclaim."

"You know a lot about them – more than I do," I

say, following her back towards reception.

"I find them interesting. I find her interesting."

Tony Vitello, the gardener, comes to get me. He's got Poppy, his little daughter, in the van and Tai, who greets me by licking my face and clambering into my lap.

"Tai," I say, cuddling him and holding his warm wiry face against my cheek. Although Poppy doesn't speak she's got a big smile and she reaches over to stroke Tai.

"All right?" says Tony, swinging the van out on to the road.

"Thanks for collecting me, and looking after Tai. What's been happening?" I ask, trying to sound grown up and not panicky like I feel inside.

Tony thinks for a moment, as if he's wondering what I can be told. "It's hard to keep track, to be honest – everyone's all up in the air. Even Dave keeps on crying, and Chris is trying to be normal, but he's at breaking point. Lady B's got very touchy, Lord B's the same. Shona, Pavel and I have searched every scrap of the greenhouses but now they know that the boy's been taken, we're all useless – which is worse than searching, to be honest. Now it's St David's and railway stations and whatnot."

"And Mum?"

Tony chews his lip slightly before answering, so I know he's not telling the whole truth. "She's – I don't rightly know."

"She's their prime suspect, isn't she?"

Tony waggles his head – he doesn't want to commit.

"She is, isn't she?"

"I dunno... She's not back, so far as I know," he says, as we bounce through puddles into the village. "Wait here. Just gonna get some smokes." And he stops suddenly, outside the post office.

Poppy reaches out to her dad as he leaves the van and her lip trembles as she looks up at me. "It's all right, Poppy," I say. "Dad will be back in a minute – don't worry."

She smiles but a single tear rolls down her creamy cheek.

I put my hands up in front of my face and play peepo with her and Tai. Soon, she's forgotten about her dad and she's happily laughing and her laughter and that drop of water on her face makes me feel the first new tear of my own. This is all horrible, like a long nightmare that won't go away.

"Hello, Poppy," says Tony, swinging back into

the van and driving on before doing up his seat belt. He turns on the radio – so that we can't talk, and I notice that even the headlines don't mention Noah.

We take the back entrance to Blackwater House. We drive over a small brick bridge and through a couple of flooded fields, and stop in the gravel yard by the potting sheds and the tractor barn in the back courtyard. Puddles are starting to form in the yard and Connor Evans has to skirt round them as he brings a pheasant feeder out of the shed and loads it into his Land Rover.

"If it keeps up like this I'll have to move the birds." He points at the sky. He's got one of his gun dogs with him. Skipper, I think it's called, and it skulks underneath the corrugated iron roof of the feed shed. Tai sniffs. Skipper sniffs. They ignore each other.

"Due to get worse," says Tony, giving him a hand with the feeder. "All right there then, Viv?" He turns to me as I stand uncertainly pulling my jacket tighter against the rain. "Shall I keep the dog?"

"Oh, no, we'll be fine now, Tony. Thank you. Bye, Poppy," I say and glance up at the back window of the flat. It's dark, so I scuttle back with Tai leaping at my ankles to the front courtyard. He races up the steps and puts his paws up against the door. But I stop outside the entrance to the flat. The door's locked and for one moment I think Mum's going to be in there, that Tony's wrong, that she has come back.

Tai whines and looks up at me, and then, the moment I open it, runs in to sniff at everything in the flat. It must smell of police people.

The flat feels very empty without Mum. Maybe Tai notices it too. He stays close to me, sitting on my feet and trotting round in small circles checking everything. "C'mon then, Tai, just the two of us," I say, and open the cupboard. Everything's in there, everything's neat, but it's all in the wrong places. The dog food has moved to the lower shelf. The Cup a Soups have swapped places with the green tea. It's like we've been burgled. For a moment I don't want to take anything – it all feels sullied – and then I reach for a sachet of noodles.

"So what if they've been here?" I ask Tai.

He growls, sniffing the air.

The kettle hasn't moved, and I set it to boil, finding a bowl and crumbling the waves of noodles into the bottom of it.

I feed Tai, even if it's the wrong time of day, top up my bowl with boiling water and sit at the kitchen table, blowing clouds of steam from the noodles. Outside, I hear footsteps on the courtyard drive and peer out. There are three police cars, Lord B's Land Rover and Chris Mumford's Land Rover. Then Chris drives off and fallen leaves dance in the empty space.

It's feeling lonely.

Wandering to the back door, I look down over the back yard. Connor Evans has gone. Poppy's playing as Tony hoses down some sheets of glass. She's stamping her wellies in the puddles and then she stops and looks up. As I watch, a policewoman appears in the yard and says something to Tony, who nods and goes to turn off the hose.

"I wonder what that was about, Tai," I say, as Tony rolls up the hosepipe. "Perhaps if we went for a walk we might find something out, or Mum might come back – while we're out?"

Tai raises one ear, looks up from his bowl and trots over to stand under his lead hanging from a hook on the back of the door.

"So you agree, do you?" I ask him.

He answers by patting the door with his paw.

I'm listening to the silence, thinking about walking, thinking about Mum, and a very tiny bit of me is also thinking about Noah, when the doorbell shrills through the flat. I consider hiding and then wonder what good that would do. Just as I'm getting to the door, it rings again, insistently enough to be quite irritating.

"I'm coming!" I shout, shuffling across the carpet with my shoes half on, half off, and find the policewoman who took my phone at the door.

"Hello, Vivienne. Would you mind coming into the house? We need to talk to everyone at the same time."

It occurs to me that they've phrased it as if I have a choice, but I haven't.

I shuffle the shoes back on, pick up my door key and follow her across the courtyard. Behind the closed door, Tai whimpers, disappointed.

I rush to catch up with her and say, "Where's Mum? When's she coming back? And can I have my phone back?"

"Oh – your mother, she's helping us with our enquiries."

"I know, but what does that mean?"

"Exactly how it sounds."

"Is it the blood? Because if it is, it's just the nosebleed he had in the car. He has loads of nosebleeds."

"I can't tell you anything at the moment," says the policewoman, pausing on the steps. "Are you all right, Vivienne? There's nothing you want to tell us – is there? I mean, do you know of anything that your mother might have been planning? We'll have to charge her soon – it's been nearly thirty-six hours."

It comes as such a shock I feel all the blood race to my face and then back to my shoes and I have to hold on to the railings to stay upright.

"Charge her?"

"Well, yes. I'm not sure exactly what the charge will be but if she's an accomplice, or even the perpetrator..."

My feet move slowly up the steps and I lurch through the doorway. The policewoman keeps talking as she ushers me on. "Anyway, Inspector Hager might be able to tell you more. Ask her about your mum."

We enter the hall. Everyone's there – everyone who lives or works on the estate, even little Poppy. There's almost no room for me to stand and I think about sitting on the sofa where Lady B is, but it's like an empty zone around her that I don't feel I can invade.

Her face is all puffy.

I stand next to Maria. She's trembling. Just a little. She takes my hand. "See you later, poppet," she says. "Pizza for supper."

Charge her.

Charge her?

I really hadn't expected that.

On my left stand the waterkeepers. Still holding Maria's hand, I try to catch Chris's eye but Ron, the other water bailiff, gets in the way. He turns his back and blocks Chris so that I can't even see his face. I shuffle closer to Maria, and she does a little smile and strokes my arm. Even she thinks Mum's not coming back, I can tell.

Sniffing back tears, I wipe my nose on my sleeve but Connor Evans pushes past me to stare out of the window and I'm forced to let go of Maria to avoid him and then she's swept away by everyone else milling around. Connor tuts and starts to text, raising his shoulder to protect his phone like I'm just a busybody nuisance. I try to get back to Maria but Sally Parsons, the dairy farm manager, plants herself right in front of me so that I can't see, and two women who work in the summer gift shop box me in completely until I'm staring at their backs. Seconds later they're joined by the man who did the bike hire last summer and then Dave from the sawmill gets up out of a chair and everyone moves around again. It's getting warm and fuggy in here, and I want to leave. I want to talk to the inspector and get out.

The door finally closes and through a gap I see Shona and Tony and Pavel from the garden, all trying to talk to the police. I look down at my feet. I feel horrible.

The buzz of conversation booms through the huge room. I can pick out some voices. Chris and Ron talk about the river. All the rain's made the banks boggy and at least two of the meadows are under water. Dave's telling Lord B about a tree down because its roots are too wet, but both of them look like they could burst into tears at any moment. The gardeners are talking about the tulips rotting. The cleaners, Olga and Natalia, are talking in Ukrainian. Connor Evans and Sally Parsons are looking out at the trees thrashing in the wind.

We all stand like we're there for a family

photograph, but nobody's smiling.

"Thank you, everybody," says a policewoman who isn't wearing a uniform and who might be Inspector Hager. "Thank you for coming in. I know you're busy, but we thought that rather than allowing gossip to spread, we'd like you all to know that we can confirm that Noah has been kidnapped."

A giant sob breaks out from the sofa in front of me and Maria rushes forward to put her arm around Lady B's shoulder. "And we have probable proof – a photograph of Noah holding an edition of a daily newspaper, today's. It appeared in the letterbox of the house first thing this morning. Hand delivered; no stamp."

Like a single being, we suck in our breath.

"This morning?" asks Dave. "How?"

"We were hoping somebody might know. Have there been any deliveries today – you know, compost for the gardens? Veg for the kitchen? Apart from Mr Vitello collecting Vivienne from school, has anyone been out?" Low-level chat starts to spread through the mass of people.

"And..." The inspector holds up a hand. "We can confirm that we are very interested in Sanjeev

Gupta, who disappeared at the same time as Noah. We'd like any information about him – although of course we'll be going to the media about this too."

At once they all start to talk – each telling their story on top of the other.

Again, the inspector holds up her hand. "Please be aware that this a very sensitive situation. Please, no posting on social media, no public speculation. We have of course advised Lord and Lady Belcombe that they shouldn't pay the ransom."

"How much is it?" calls Connor Evans.

"That's not something anyone needs to know—"

"But we are raising it anyway," interrupts Lord B. "My brother Peregrine has agreed to help us because of course Noah is very important – he is the last of the line, the last of the..." He breaks down and Lady B grips his arm and they both look at the floor.

The policewoman who came to the house and a policeman I hadn't noticed before move in to record everyone as they begin to talk, and no one pays any attention to me.

"Hey!" I say. "What about Mum? When's Mum coming back?" I shout into the storm of voices but nobody seems to hear me. "Listen to me," I yell into the mass of people surging towards Inspector Hager. "Please – what's happening about my mum? Are you going to charge her? Has she got a lawyer?"

The inspector looks at me. Maybe she sees my age; maybe she sees my school uniform. Whatever, she doesn't answer me, she just starts noting down something that Shona says.

"What?" I say. "What about me? What about Mum?"

I give it a minute, five perhaps, before turning and slamming the door and marching out into the garden.

They didn't want me. They didn't notice me.

They don't care.

Chapter 9

It's been so wet for so long that the edges of the lawn are falling away into a kind of swamp, and the rain's actually causing ripples between the blades of grass.

Without thinking, I've ended up at the bottom of the main lawn, my shoes squidging into the turf, springs bursting out all around my feet, drowned worms caught in the waterlog.

I glance back up towards the house. The tall windows shine blankly back at the sky. I can't see it at all, but I'd bet they're all still in there, talking. I bet no one's even noticed that I've gone.

"Damn you, Noah Belcombe! Damn you and damn your whole horrible family! Damn this place!" I shout, and a duck takes off in a panic, flapping away upriver.

A scraggy goat willow hangs over the river and I pick my way to it through the waterlogged grass, clambering up the long horizontal trunk so that I can sit, hanging over the river as it charges past beneath me.

Surges of anger and then panic race through my chest. How dare they all ignore me? How dare they ignore Mum?

But what's going to happen to me if Mum doesn't come back?

All the stories I've ever heard about wrongful convictions race through my mind. People have served really long prison sentences for crimes they didn't commit. Loads of investigations go wrong because the police don't get all the evidence at the beginning.

Why did I have to punch stupid Noah?

Why did his stupid nose have to bleed all over the stupid car?

Why did he have to be such an idiot? If he was a reasonable human being we'd never have got into a fight.

"Ugh!" I shout at the river, and this time a coot takes off, calling with each beat of her wing.

"Stupid!" I shout at the top of my lungs and the crows in the beech trees burst into the air, circling and landing, circling and landing.

I try to calm myself by watching the river. Every second the surface changes. Whorls of water curl around the centre of the stream, black from the dead leaves lining the gravel bottom.

This was always a good place to sit. On very hot days, Daisy and I would hang from the main branch, letting our legs dangle into the icy river, until the current took us and our hands slipped and we bounced downstream, our bums catching on the chalk-pebbled mud banks, our hands scrabbling at the boards that held back the banks.

When it was too cold to swim, we pretended to fish here. A hook, some line and a twig. Nothing caught, but hours of fiddling and rearranging. Once, Chris taught us how to tickle a trout.

"You need a bramble, and a lot of patience."

He brought one out that day. A rainbow trout, silver and spotted and clear-eyed, which wriggled and flipped on the bank until I begged him to throw it back. It swam the instant it hit the water and we watched it laze in the current, swishing its tail left and right, effortless.

Then there were the waterweed islands. Huge rafts of festering green stuff that formed over days after the waterkeepers had trimmed back the plumes of fresh green waterweed in the river. Moorhens would try to nest in it and ducks would sit on top as it floated downstream. Under the mill bridge it wedged beneath a low sewer pipe and Chris and Ron would wade into the stream and tug at it with giant rakes until the huge fizzing, stinking island broke loose and bobbed in the water, gaining speed and crashing into the packhorse bridge further on. Then they'd thrash at it and we'd help, grappling with rakes, tearing it apart, breaking it until it whizzed away to get caught on someone else's weed rack.

Noah would never help. He'd just watch, all perfect in his white socks, from the riverbank. Him and Herbert. We had such a good time, but was he wishing he could join in? I wonder.

Just now, the river's so full and so cold, I can't imagine that anything would get stuck under the sewer pipe, or that anything would want to build a nest. Looking down from here in my tree I can see the water running fast through the lawn grass. The river's spread so much even in the time I've been sitting here.

Shuffling round I turn to face the house. I don't expect anyone can see me here. The goat willow's leaves have gone but the twigs are dense and give a good cover. Upstream, the riverbank's dotted with willows and small outcrops of hawthorn, but just now the footpaths that line each bank have disappeared so that the river seems to run right into the fields. Some cows stand ankle-deep, drinking from the water that's appeared by their feet. The rain intensifies and the smell of woodsmoke drifts across the lawn. They've lit the fire in the house. The day's fading and without my anger to keep me warm it's getting cold.

There's just a chance that they've brought Mum back, although there's been no actual sign. No cars. I don't want to go back to find the flat empty again but I'm getting very wet.

I go back to the empty flat.

* * *

Soon, the giant puddle in the centre of the stable courtyard will form.

The rainwater drains will overfill and the river will come right up to the house.

I should be settling in with Maria in the kitchen, like a servant, but I don't want to be in the kitchen with Maria and anyway, Tai needs a walk. Tai deserves a walk.

So I put on my raincoat and head out. They can't get hold of me, I haven't got a phone – still. And I don't owe any of them anything. If I choose to disappear then bad luck to them. None of them have got Mum back. They're not even trying to get Mum back.

I hate them all.

"All except you, Tai." I run my hand the length of his back, comforted by his warmth. "All except you."

Grabbing his lead, we slip out of the back door down to the stable courtyard and into the rain. It patters on my face, tapping on my hood. The orchard, usually sweet with fermenting apple juice, just smells cold and wet, and the heaps of fruit sit blackly by the path, late autumn slugs gorging themselves on the rotting pulp.

From the orchard, the ground is squelchy and it takes a while to reach the dark hedges that line the rose garden. Wet wind roars through the valley, playing between the hedges and beating my coat around my legs. This must be the storm that Chris mentioned yesterday. Tai gallops off after a squirrel and charges back, squeezing through a gap in the yew and then returning, a stick in his mouth.

I throw it, once, twice, three times, until we're on the edge of the formal garden, heading towards the orange clouds of beech trees massing up the hillside.

In front of us, in the heart of the woods, an early owl hoots. Behind us, a distant someone starts a car.

"Which way, Tai?" He leaps as I throw the stick and he charges off into Folly Wood, galloping through the beeches, hunting smells and rabbits between the huge grey tree trunks.

Somewhere a long way back, a door bangs. A woman's voice calls. It might be my name, but it doesn't sound like Mum's voice so I ignore it and turn out of the garden, following Tai, picking my way along the path that in summer is wide and filled with birdsong. Now it's deep with the fallen leaves. They form a carpet that dances like orange handprints all around my feet, still bright even on the ground.

The rain falls so heavily that beyond my hood I can hear it hammering on the woodland floor. A blackbird cries as I approach and the crows answer.

Picking up speed, I stomp under the trees, swinging around the bend so that the house disappears behind me. Overhead, the branches wave and beech leaves still fall. Tai races off from the path, chasing the leaves as they spiral down and thundering through drifts of fallen ones, throwing up bursts of reds and yellows. He disappears for minutes at a time and then charges back towards me. We pass a giant yew we used to hide in and the donkey hut with the metal tank that Noah dared me to climb inside, but luckily Chris rescued me before I clambered in – or I probably would have died in there as it was taller than me and full of stinky water. Typical Noah.

Tai bombs across the logging path and bursts out of the woodland and I follow until I'm in the meadows that run along the river.

"Stupid idiot!" I say out loud. "Stupid family!" I remember Lord B's furious outburst and shudder. "Like it's my fault I was trying to find your scabby son." Kicking a molehill, I stamp on through the wet field, muttering to myself. "And why aren't you helping me get my mum back?" I say, sticking mental pins in Lord B's imaginary effigy. "Why aren't you being the adult? I'm just a kid." I've got so many emotions fighting for air I have to sniff back the tears and walk faster to drive them away.

It's boggy underfoot but a ridge of chalk runs through the field and I've walked it so many times I find it easily in the gloom. Two stiles later and I'm wondering about turning back. We're almost at the edge of the estate and Tai keeps stopping to sniff the air and look behind us as if we're leaving his territory. Quite soon the path will reach the lane where the blackberry bushes grow high on both sides. It'll be even darker there. I pause, listening to the rain on my hood, and look back towards the woods. It's beginning to look creepy under the trees. To my right, the river still reflects the sky, steely and cold, with apricot sunset streaks. Here, the river splits. One side is the weir, with a plank bridge that crosses it. In the middle is a small island, which is the ancient fulling mill site, the mill itself gone, long before I was born. It was something to do with cloth, I think. But just now, the island has almost disappeared, marked only by a hut and an old wild pear tree. On the far side is another plank bridge that crosses the actual mill race, a narrow strip of scarily fast and dangerous water, even when it's not in flood. It's where the water wheel used to be. There are still a load of giant iron cogs lying on the river bed, the remains of the mechanism. Upstream is the flat grey mill pond. An expanse of apparently still water that in the summer we always wanted to swim in but Mum said was too dangerous. Just now it looks very cold.

Downstream the river becomes one, an enormous mass of grey thundering down towards the house and Alchester.

I stand on the footpath and stare across at the island, watching the water consuming it. Something moves on the edge of the plank bridge. Something's caught. A bird?

I peer harder – no, it's a cat. Tigger? Stuck on the island. He doesn't want to cross the bridge.

At the same time, Tai spots him and begins to bark.

"Shh, boy, shhh. Tigger's scared; you'll make him scareder."

Tai doesn't care and goes on barking. He races to the bridge and barks again. Tigger retreats to the pear tree.

"Don't go up it!" I say out loud. Tigger, the most fearless cat in the world, crouches, terrified.

For a moment the rain stops, although the wind doesn't.

"Stay, Tai," I say in my most severe voice. "Wait." I point a finger at the ground and Tai sits. The second I leave, he rises to all fours again. "Stay," I say again. He sits again, panting, little barks bursting out all over the place.

There's a coot calling somewhere on the water. A pair of ducks swoosh on to the mill pond to sleep for the night, safely out of the reach of foxes, and Tigger looks over to me and mews. I head towards the first bridge. The river's so high that when I reach it, it's brushing the underside of the planks, oozing through the wood and pooling on the surface. There should be a drop in water level to my right, below the weir, but the river's almost flat, there's so much water. I wonder if the level's still rising. I know that flooding doesn't happen instantly, that it can take hours to reach its highest point.

I completely understand why the cat doesn't want to cross. I'm not sure I want to cross.

Behind me, Tai lets out a string of barks.

I watch the water for a minute. It's rising. Fast.

In the gloom I take a moment to work out if the second bridge is going to be crossable. I don't want to get trapped here.

Grasping the slimy wooden rail, I walk carefully over the water. It boils and hisses on both sides, so fast and so powerful that I nearly turn back. But in three paces, I'm across.

The ground is spongy underfoot, breathing water out as I press down with my feet, and I try to forget that in the past I've actually seen the island disappear under the water. Completely.

"Here, Tigger," I say, but I don't really need to say anything because he leaps into my arms, jamming his head beneath my chin, under the hood. "What on earth are you doing here? Where did you come from?"

I stand under the bare branches of the pear tree watching the water skim over the second bridge. It's not as safe as I thought; in fact, I'm not sure it's going to be possible to cross.

"We'll have to go back the way we came. I hope it's the right side of the river for you, Tigger."

As I wade to the bridge clutching the cat under my right arm, the rain starts again, lashing sideways under my hood. I shuffle really slowly over the wire-netting-covered boards.

Careful, Viv.

"Nearly there," I say, wondering how far from the river I can leave the cat. He mews and claws at my coat. In front of me the trickle of water crossing the bridge becomes a rush, and behind me a racing roar as it thunders over the old mill workings.

And something else. Thumping?

Banging?

I turn and listen, but Tai starts to bark again.

"Shh, Tai," I say. Over the water's roar it's hard to make anything out, exactly – but there's definitely something thumping, and I don't think it's a log caught in the weir.

"Hello!" I shout. There's nowhere for anyone to be – I can see around everything. There's only the shed itself.

I splash on to the grass, moving away from the bridge and back towards the woods until I'm on solid ground. Tigger seems to know when to leap, and twists from my arm, landing neatly on the grass and trotting off into the gloom without a backward glance. Tai lunges towards him but I grab his collar and listen.

Nothing.

"Hello!" I shout, back towards the shed.

Thump.

Thump.

Thump.

Quickly, I turn and wade back over the bridge until I'm on the island. This time, Tai follows me.

Thump.

Thump.

Thump.

"I think it's coming from the shed, Tai."

Thump.

Thump.

Thump.

Tai starts barking hard. Backing away from the shed, he ends up dog-knee-deep in the water and leaps forward, barking even more.

It could be an animal – but would an animal beat so evenly on the side?

Noah?

Could it be?

I walk right up to the shed, my feet almost out of the water.

"Noah?" I call into the tiny gap at the bottom of the shed.

For about ten seconds the banging comes back frantically.

"What? It *is* you?" Instinctively I reach into my pocket – of course, no phone. No one's going to come and help me get him out.

Mixed feelings crowd into my head. Part of me wants to leave him in there, because after all, what do I owe him? But the grown-up side of me knows he's in real danger of drowning and we have to get him out.

"But how, Tai. How?"

I glance at the river. The second bridge is very definitely under fast water and now my feet are actually splashing in the grass. I could run all the way back to the house through the woods – it would take me half an hour at least, but in half an hour the island might be completely under water. Tai turns and trots away from me back over the bridge. His feet splash as he goes. He must know something about this, like how long we have until the island disappears.

"Hang on!" I shout, racing around the outside of the shed. The back is very nearly submerged, the river lapping at the corrugation. The door at the end is fastened with a huge shiny padlock. I pull at it in the desperate hope that it might give way. It doesn't.

"I'm gonna get you out," I shout again. "It's just I don't have my phone, the police took it." The corrugated iron is strong and goes top to bottom with no apparent way of levering it off. Hooking my fingers under the side I try to pull, but nothing moves.

The thumping comes again from inside.

Beneath my feet, the water is creeping across the whole island, covering everything but the tallest blades of grass.

Now, on the other side of the river, Tai barks and dances madly in the watery grass.

"I know, Tai, but you're not helping."

Noah thumps again. I'm guessing the water's appeared inside the shed too now.

"Yes, yes," I say. Splashing over to the mill race and feeling the ground around the hatches above it, I search for an iron bar that ought to be there because it's used to open and close the hatches. All the hatches on the estate have iron bars with hooks in the end to raise and lower the huge wooden gates that control the flow. They're usually just lying in the grass. If you know where to look. With the water rising around my wrists, I fumble all around where the bank should be. It would be perfect – I could lever off a sheet of the corrugated iron – but there's nothing there, just masses of ice-cold water that within seconds has covered my ankles.

"Doing my best," I call. Both the plank bridges have vanished. They're marked by the rails but there's no other sign that they're even there.

Tai's still barking, but he's quite a long way back from the water now. He knows it's going to flood.

It's also very nearly dark. This is getting scary.

Noah thumps again.

"Stop it – you're not helping either. I'm not going to leave you but I can't find a way in." The roots of the pear tree are out of the water and among them I spy a short iron bar. Perhaps that's what I'm looking for, in which case it's shorter than I remember, but I can't find anything to lever it against except for my foot and the ground's so squishy it just sinks in.

"Argh!" I throw the bar down. It bounces against the side of the hut and disappears under the water.

Noah thumps on the walls again. "Yes – I know!" I shout. "I'm still here, still trying."

And then I see the ladder. "Hang on," I say.

Leaning against the other side of the pear tree is a fruit ladder – old but solid – and I pull it against the shed. Four rungs up and I can see the roof panels properly, and they're not as secure as the walls.

In almost complete darkness I feel for a gap and slip my fingers into it, pulling and pulling until there's a pinging sound and the whole sheet comes loose and I can drag it across.

"Yes!" I say, peering down into the darkness. "Noah?"

A pale blob looks up towards me. "Mmmm," it says.

The roof is slippery, and the runnels of the corrugation are full of black crumbly stuff that sticks all over my hands but I make it to the top of the ladder and balance on the top of the wall.

Noah – because it is Noah; I can see the blond mane – shakes his head. "Mmm – mmmm," he says.

"What?" I say, almost enjoying the fact that he can't speak.

"Mmm, mmmm," he says with urgency.

I glance behind me. There's no one here – why's he warning me?

"I'm coming down," I say, swinging my legs into the gap and squeezing through. There's a moment as my feet dangle when I could change my mind and climb out, and that's when I realise that the reason Noah's shaking his head is that we won't be able to get out again. Even with a hole in the roof.

I grab at the corrugations above my head, trying to haul myself up, but there's no grip and my fingers slide across the roof.

Flump.

I land in the water, in almost complete darkness. There's a triangle of dark sky above me and the faint silhouette of Noah's head.

Chapter 10

"Well at least I can untie you," I say, ripping off the tape that's been stuck over his mouth.

"Ow!" he squawks. "Ow! Well, that was intelligent. Now you've completely blown our chances of getting out of here."

"Oh, yeah?" I say. "Well, I might just slap another piece of tape over your gob and leave you to rot."

"You might as well have done. You're a total idiot, you know that?!"

"What?"

"*More* than averagely idiotic, I'd say, actually, because any other deadhead would have noticed that climbing into a box without a way out was fatheadedly unthinking."

I'm almost impressed by his insults. Luckily he can't see my face.

"I'm a complete idiot?" I say. "*You're* the idiot – getting yourself kidnapped! And you could at least say thank you to me for trying to help you."

"Oh, yeah, thanks. Thanks a bunch for nothing. And – *like* I did this on purpose! You think I wanted to be kidnapped? And why have the police got your phone?"

"Because they have. And perhaps you did want to be kidnapped. Perhaps, somehow, you got yourself kidnapped – just so that your dumb lord and lady whatnot parents would sit and weep buckets—"

"Are they?" interrupts Noah. "Weeping, I mean?"

"Yeah. And the whole estate's running round like ants trying to find you – except for Mum."

"Why not Marion? I'd have thought she might actually be quite upset if I was kidnapped."

My anger vanishes and suddenly I feel sad and actually quite afraid. "Mum's been arrested – or something. I haven't seen her for two days. The police took her. They think she kidnapped you – with Sanjeev."

But Noah hasn't caught my change of mood. "Oh, how simply *dreadful* for you. I've been kidnapped, living in sheds, weeing in a bucket – and now I'm going to drown. And you haven't seen your mum for two days but at least you know that she's tucked up safe and sound in a police station. I could have been dead for all you knew. And who's Sanjeev?"

"Your PE teacher. And actually we'll both be dead soon," I say. "We're both going to drown if we don't get out of here."

Noah draws in a breath as if he's going to say something and stops.

"Are we really?" he asks. "Where are we?"

"At the remains of the fulling mill – in the middle of the river. The river that's burst its banks."

He pauses. "It's reached my ankles, like, really fast," he says. "Thing is, Viv," and his voice goes all serious, "although you can undo my hands, I'm attached to the shed."

"How, attached?" I ask, picking at the rope around his wrists.

In answer he shuffles and I hear the clank of a chain.

"Chained?" I say. "Seriously?"

"It's an old-fashioned actual shackle, I think,

around my ankle."

"Oh, my god that's, like, so ancient history," I say crouching down and fumbling around in the dark, feeling his feet under the water. I find a ring padlocked around his ankle; it's as thick as my thumb. I chase the chain to the side of the hut where it's padlocked to a huge metal loop coming out of the floor. I let out a long sigh.

"You can't undo it, can you?"

I shake my head, then realise that he can't see me.

"We're going to die here," he says, his voice quite cold.

"Nah," I say. "You're too valuable, aren't you? They'll be back. And listen to Tai – he's not going to stop barking until we get out of here."

"Dunno," he says in the end. "I've never seen them, you know. Never heard them speak. Even though I've asked them questions. Perhaps they don't care."

For a moment, I don't say anything. Tai *is* barking. He's barking his head off; surely someone at the house can hear him. Surely. "Was that photo real – you know, of you and the newspaper?" The rope on his hands is wet and swollen, but it loosens and soon it falls in the water at our feet.

"Yeah – it was scary. They sat me on a chair, handed me a paper and I stared at a mobile phone while they took pictures."

"Where were you?"

"In a shed – a different shed. I've been in a lot of sheds. Oh, that feels better..." He rubs his hands together.

"Who do you think it is?" I ask, trying to sound cheerful and normal and feeling along the bottom of the shed. The water is actually flowing in quite fast. My wellingtons are only just tall enough.

Noah sighs. "I don't know – they're big. Men. They never speak. I've never seen them."

"What d'you mean, you haven't seen them?" I run my hands around every inch of the walls, searching for anything that isn't smooth iron. Anything that I could use as a lever. I'm going to keep him talking. He's scared, I can hear it in his voice, and me keeping him calm is keeping me calm.

"I haven't seen their faces. They wear balaclavas – and gloves. They wear them all the time."

"How often do they come?" I have a sudden thought and try and orientate myself, peering up through the hole in the roof until I can see the pear tree.

"Once a day – sometimes morning, sometimes evening. I think they've been here for today. They fed me some soup. They moved me here last night. Before that, I was in another shed. I've no idea where that was – not by the river though."

"Uh-huh," I say, kneeling on the floor of the shed and letting the icy water flow into my wellingtons. I begin to claw at the floorboards, which are softer than I'm expecting. Long splinters of wood come away in my hands.

"What are you trying to do – dig our way out? In case you haven't noticed, the ground's under water? *Duh*?"

"You could help me," I say. "And I'm not digging my way out – I'm trying to reach something that's outside on the ground. If I'm right we might be able to grab the iron bar that I dropped outside a few minutes ago. It must be really close."

Tai's barking steps up a pace. He now sounds completely frantic. "Oh, Tai," I mumble.

"I wish I'd had him when I was taken," says Noah. "They'd never have got me."

Although we manage to pull the wood of the flooring away, digging is much harder, and made harder still by the rising water. We've barely made an impression before the water's at my armpits and I have to pull my head up to breathe.

"It's not going to happen," says Noah. "I think you should get out – I could lift you up – and try and get help."

"I'll keep going, at least for a bit," I say.

I don't say, *You might drown while I'm getting it.* If this island floods properly, even the pear tree will end up underwater.

Noah doesn't answer – but I sense him moving faster, just as the cold and wet begin to get to me and I slow down.

Then the water gets so high that we actually have to dive under.

And we haven't even cleared enough room under the wall of the shed to reach outside.

We both stop, and stand and breathe.

"Thank you," he says. "I think I should say it, in case."

"We'll be fine," I say and, taking a deep breath, I drop to my knees, jamming my hand under the shed, willing it to go forward. A stone bashes my wrist, probably taking some skin off, and I force my forearm through the soil, but I'm running out of breath so I have to pull back to stand. But I can't – my arm won't come through the gap.

Pull! My body screams. *Pull!*

I pull.

My arm won't move. I'm stuck. Oh, god, I'm going to drown with my arm stuck under a shed wall rescuing someone I hate.

And then Noah's pulling me, yanking at my arm, his fingernails scrabbling to free my hand and we lunge backwards, both falling against the far side of the shed, our heads just above the water.

We breathe. I listen to our breaths, the roar of the water, the slap of the rain on the roof. Tai, barking himself hoarse.

"Thank you," I say. "Thank you."

"S'all right," he says. "How close were you to getting your hand outside?"

"Near," I say. "Very near."

"OK?" he asks, and we dive down. I feel him pull away the stone and I thrust my arm through, my hand breaking through to feel the soft muddy grass outside. I reach as far as I can, getting my shoulder under the side of the shed and patting the ground until I feel the hard cold steel of the iron bar.

Chapter 11

It's not easy to get it back, I have to take three plunges to pull it against the side of the shed, and then Noah manages to get it sideways so that we can feed it through, and then it jams and then finally he stands with it in his hands.

Now the water's waist-high, and the sides of the shed are being buffeted by it.

"Do you think the whole thing could end up being washed downstream?" he asks.

"Don't think about it," I answer, diving down and putting one end of the bar inside the padlock that attaches the chain to the floor.

"Is this going to work?" he asks.

"Of course," I say, sounding a million times more confident than I feel.

We both lean on the bar. Once, twice, three times, each time the stupid thing just bounces out.

"I'll try the other end," I say, and dive down again to jam it into the loop of the padlock.

For a second time, we both lean. Something gives, and then something gives again and I plunge under the water to find the padlock hanging loose.

"Yeah!" I stand up, holding the end of the chain in my hand. "You're free – now, let's get out of here."

* * *

The thing about being really cold is that you can't feel much. Also, you can't really control your muscles. I think I thought that it would be quite easy for Noah to lift me up to the roof and for me to climb out. I'm tiny, and he's quite tall. It should be easy.

But he doesn't seem to be able to lift very well and my arms have frozen so that they feel like marshmallows. It takes four attempts and some rude words to get me up to the roof – and then I wonder just how I'm going to pull him up.

I peer down into the hole where I know he must be.

"Pass me the bar," I say.

There's some splashing below and the iron bar appears through the hole. I use it to lever another panel off the roof and then, balanced on the wall, I reach down for the ladder and, fighting the horizontal rain, manage to post its legs into the shed.

"Yes!" says Noah, and I hear him clambering out, his feet awkward on the rungs, his iron shackle clanging against the wood.

Soon he's sitting alongside me on the roof and we both start to shake, the deep cold of the water replaced by the icy wind and rain of the world outside.

"Dark, isn't it," he stammers.

"Yes." I can't actually see Tai any more. I can only hear him, his barks desperate above the roar of the storm.

"Only wearing my school uniform," he says.

"Uh," I say back. I'm wearing a wet coat and wet jeans. Socks but no shoes; I lost the wellies in the shed. Nothing about me is dry. Or warm.

"We quite badly need to get off this island," I say. "The water's really deep and I don't know if the shed will stand it."

"Hmm," he says, and he slides down the roof in front of the shed and I hear his feet splash into the water.

"Oh, god – it's cold," he calls.

"Is it safe down there?"

"Yes," he calls up to me. "Water's quite still just here."

For a second I think about trust, and Noah, and how the two almost never go together. I let go and slip slowly from the corrugations, dropping into the water, the soft earth of the island breaking my fall.

We stand waist-deep in the dark water. Shuddering with the cold. The rain goes from hard wet rain to lashing rain, making me even colder.

We are literally standing in the middle of the river. Out of the current, but still in the middle of the river.

"Can you see the bridge at all?" I ask.

There's a long silence and then Noah says, "No. I can't."

"OK – take my hand," I say, and with my frozen

socked feet, squinting against the rain dripping over my face, I wade across the island, into the current, dragging him towards where I think the bridge might be. The flow is so strong, my feet are pushed away each time I take a step and I have less and less confidence about where we're heading. Halfway to where it should be he stops. "Why don't we use the ladder and sit in the tree? We could wait it out?"

I stop pulling on his hand and try to think, although it's getting harder to think because I'm so cold and my brain seems to have stopped working.

"Er…" I try to remember why he's wrong. Why we have to make it off the island. "I think we'd die of exposure." That's it – I'm so cold, I need to get somewhere warm. "We'd be there all night. And…" I recall why I panicked. "Do you remember when we were little, the tree was under the water? Ducks clinging to the top of it?"

I wait while Noah's brain works it out.

"Is this going to work, Viv?"

"Maybe," I say.

We begin to walk again. Not only are my feet washing sideways, they're heavy. It's like when you have a dead leg and you know your foot must have hit the ground but the rest of your body doesn't seem to have got the message – but even weirder.

I slap my foot against the grass and feel solid wood beneath my toes. Despite the water being waist-deep, I'm reassured.

"Here," I say, bringing Noah's hands on to the railing. "Hold on to that."

"Oh!" he says, and I can hear the relief in his voice.

Tai's barking lessens. Perhaps he can see us. "S'all right, Tai, we're coming back," I shout.

For a second, we stop, both of us gripping the rail, both of us breathing heavily. "So we go across the bridge, take the path over the water meadows, and through the woods. We could be home in half an hour."

"With crumpets," he says.

"With a warm bath."

"With fluffy towels and soup and a flushing toilet."

"Yeah," I say, wondering why I don't quite feel it's going to happen. "Ready?"

I slide my right foot along the plank, *one, two,* and then I step again. "Only one plank," I yell. The water's dragging my foot to the side. I wonder if we're able to cross here. It might be too dangerous.

I rock forwards and backwards, moving my weight from one foot to the other.

It should be possible.

Noah bumps against me, gripping my arm. "What's happened to the other one?" is what I think he says as the remaining plank is swept away under my foot. I plunge into the river and I feel the air forced out of my lungs, the icy water closing over my head. The current drags me downstream. My hand tightens on the rail and I hang on. Icy prickles rush up from my feet, through my legs, into my arms, numbing my hands so that I can't feel if they're holding on to the wood or not. My clothes, my legs, everything is trying to whisk me away from the rail I'm hanging on to.

"No!" I hear Noah yelling from somewhere above my head. "Viv!" he shouts.

"Here," I say, forcing my head up, still clutching the railing. "Grab."

His arm reaches mine and we grasp each other.

It takes a few seconds to work out that he's on the remains of the bridge, but can't cross any further, and I'm being held in the stream by a piece of rotting wood and a single nail. It feels as if my coat is alive and actively trying to drown me and I try to shuffle it off my shoulders and all the while I'm struggling to breathe while my body's having a panic attack.

He pulls me and I let go of the rail, grabbing the post that's still sticking out of the water until I'm right up close to him and we're both perched in the middle of the stream, the force of the current so strong that I can't imagine how I ever thought we could cross the bridge.

"Thank you," I mutter.

"This is hopeless," he says, which is when the headlights appear on the other side of the river.

* * *

In the darkness, I can't really work out what's going on, but soon a white shape appears on the water, upstream of the broken bridge – and it can float. On top of it there's a figure holding a torch, but through the rain I can't work out who they are. They shout something, which is taken off on the wind, and then the white boat bumps up against the remains of the bridge and without anyone saying a word, we launch ourselves inside, shuddering and shaking and mumbling "thank you"s into the storm. The boat's an inflatable and floats us over what should be fields all the way to the woods.

Probably a police boat. "Funny that they keep one," I say to the wind.

I'm vaguely surprised to see that the vehicle parked on the bank isn't covered in reflective police markings, but I don't really think about it as someone throws open the back of a dimly lit van and we stumble into the dark, shivering, Tai yapping and growling alongside us.

"Well done, boy," I say. "You raised the alarm." I run my shuddering frozen fingers through his fur and he growls again. "Shh," I say. "Shh now, boy, we're rescued. It's over." While I peel off my wet socks and struggle out of my jeans and try to dry my legs with a blanket picked off a pile of dry bedding in the corner, Tai licks my face. I feel myself relaxing, almost into sleep, until a dark shape lunges forward and yanks Tai out by the collar, slamming the door.

"What?" I shout.

Tai barks, then yowls and there's a thud, followed by a whine, and then the engine starts up.

"What? What's happening? Where's Tai?"

Alongside me I hear Noah peeling wet clothes from his skin and, like me, wrapping himself in blankets. "What d'you mean?" he asks, as the tyres slip on the wet leaves and we're thrown back and forth.

"They've just done something to Tai – and this is not right," I say, suddenly wide awake and realising that we're turning the wrong way and that we don't seem to be heading back towards the house. Whatever we're driving over is rough. We must be heading through the woods.

"What?" says Noah. "Jesus, I can't get warm."

"Stop," I say. "Don't take your clothes off – this isn't a rescue."

As I say it, something makes the driver swerve and I'm flung across the blankets.

"They're not taking us home, and they threw Tai out of the van and..." I can't say it. That thud, that noise, it didn't sound good, and the tiny whine that came afterwards... "Get your clothes back on. Something's really wrong."

"What? What the...?"

I struggle to pull my jeans back up my legs. They're so wet, and my legs are so cold, and my hands have no grip – it's agony. Once I've got them on I try to get my socks back on but I can only find one.

Alongside me Noah's swearing at his clothes, and

I imagine a wet school uniform is no better.

"Where are we going?" I shout over the sound of the engine, but I doubt the driver can hear us.

"So far we've turned left," says Noah. "We should be passing through the village."

"Oh, yeah?" I say.

"I got pretty good at this," he says. "They moved me about six times."

I skid across the bottom of the van as we swing to the right and my shoulder crashes into the wooden lining. "Ow!"

"Hang on to the metal bits," Noah says. "Above the plywood – honestly, they're easier."

Crouching, I take his advice and cling to the framework. At least this way my fingerprints are being left behind.

"We should have stayed put," he says.

"And died of exposure?"

"Might have been better than this," he says, as we lurch again.

"I suppose there's no possibility that this is a weird kind of rescue mission," I say.

There's a long silence and he says, "No, I don't think there is."

Chapter 12

Eventually, we turn down another bumpy track and stop. Somebody does something with a metal gate or a metal fence, then the van lurches forwards again before stopping a second time. There's a kind of silence, a "trees thrashing in the wind and rain beating on the roof" kind of silence, and the doors on both side of the cab slam. Feet crunch on gravel and the back door is flung open before a very powerful torch beam shines in on us. Its light catches the twin barrels of what I recognise is a shotgun.

"S'OK – we're not going to do anything," I say,

almost unable to speak. Cold or fear? I can't tell.

The torch retreats and the person holding it shines it at a shed. It's a much bigger shed than the one we were in before and this one's not surrounded by water.

"I think they want us to go there," says Noah, shuffling towards the doors of the van.

"OK," I say, "that's what we'll do." My words sound ridiculous – in fact my voice sounds ridiculous but I really don't know how else to react.

Grabbing the remaining blankets from the van, I follow Noah through the rain over pointy gravel towards a large white door that's standing open. Inside, there's a low light and we walk towards it. The moment we've gone through the doorway, the door slams behind us and I hear bolts sliding across.

"Where's Tai?" I shout. "I want my dog, Tai."

"Hey!" shouts Noah. "Hey!" But no one answers.

I run to the window, hoping to get a glimpse of the van, but it's been boarded up on the outside and all I can do is listen through the hammering rain as the engine surges, the metal gates clang, and then the sound of a motor gradually dies away.

I sink to my heels, breathing hard, trying to blink

away the tears of fright that have caught me by surprise.

"That was scary," says Noah, slumping alongside me, clutching his knees to his chest.

"And they took Tai." My voice fades as I say his name.

"They had a gun," he mutters.

I stop thinking about Tai and listen to what he says. "A shotgun."

"Like it makes a difference."

"They're local." My mouth says it although I didn't know my brain was thinking it.

"Like how? Don't people in other parts of the country have shotguns?"

"It wasn't like, sawn off – it was like clay pigeon shooting. I don't think people in London have shotguns. I don't think they need them. Also, how would a London person know about that shed?"

"Maybe," he says, slowly peeling off his socks. "Whatever. I'm not going to be able to get my trousers off because of this stupid chain."

"Did they have a gun when they grabbed you?"

"Oh, god, I don't know. Look, can we just try and get warm?"

Shoving big thoughts to the side of my mind I

try to be practical and not let myself think about what's happening to us. I examine the room for the first time. It's a longish shed, this time plastered on the inside, like a proper room. The dim light comes from a single lightbulb hanging from the ceiling. In the corner is a cardboard box on top of some mangy cushions and along one wall there's a big chest freezer, which is humming slightly. The room smells of damp and the brown carpet feels oily under my bare feet. It's kind of like a Scout hut or something, but I can't think of any Scout huts anywhere near us. Sure that they've gone, I risk undressing. Shakily, I get to my feet and tug off my sopping coat and soaking wet sweater. I wrap a blanket around my top half then, under cover of that, I unpeel my jeans for the second time. It actually feels colder without them and my legs are eerily pale and flocked with goose pimples.

"Is that a blow heater?" says Noah, pointing to the wall from beneath the tent of blankets he's wrapped around his top half.

"I dunno," I say, investigating the white thing attached to the plaster. It has *on* and *off* switches. I press *on*, and a red light appears. Nothing much else happens. "No," I say. "But it might be another kind of heater – I don't know what else it could be. Let's move about. It'll help us get warm."

Both of us shuffle around the space, our blankets hanging down to the floor. I can't actually feel my feet or hands but I know it's the middle of your body that matters. As I walk, I notice more about the room. There's a piece of plywood tacked over what could be a fireplace, and a door at the far end, which I assume is locked, but when I pass it and flick down the handle – it opens.

"Wow!" says Noah.

It's warmer than the room we're in, definitely. The dim light doesn't do much in the extra space so I flap my hands around searching for a light switch. Something bounces against my face – a light pull. I grab at it and tug. A small strip light pings into life and I see that it's a storeroom with another freezer, switched on but locked. It's this that must be warming the room. Then there are some shelves and, best of all, a lavatory.

"Yay!" shouts Noah behind me. "Mine!"

He charges past and slams the door, so I resume my march, swinging my arms, willing my blood to warm up. In passing, I run my hand over the maybe-heater and am rewarded with a slight warmth, which must be new. Should I hang our wet clothes on it or press our freezing bodies to it? In the end I decide the clothes need to win. With difficulty, I drape my jeans over the end, and my sock across the middle. I wish I had the other sock. I wish I still had my wellies.

I'm trying really hard to be sensible about this but the thought that we're now in a worse position than we were in when we were waist-deep in the flood keeps creeping back and freezing my head.

Noah comes out of the storeroom. "I wouldn't go in there for a bit," he says, hopping from one foot to the other, the chain around his leg clanking. Now that I can see it properly I can't imagine how we're going to get it off without a key.

"Thanks," I say. "You seem very calm about all this."

"Well, it's all a lot better than it was five hours ago."

"Is it?"

"I was on my own, in a shed filling with water, chained to the wall – and no toilet."

Five hours ago I was eating a noodle soup in a warm flat with a dog.

Oh, Tai. Poor Tai. I imagine him lying on the side of the river, the water rising. *Don't think about it.*

This morning feels a lifetime ago.

"What are we going to do, Noah?" I say. "They've got guns, we've got nothing – not even shoes."

He rubs his feet with the blanket and arranges his socks on the heater.

"D'you remember we used to play games where you had the gun and I had the sword and we fought and – and it was fun … and we trusted each other."

"Hmm," he says, and I see his eyes fill and suddenly everything goes blurry and I realise that I'm crying too. I wipe the tears away with the back of my hand and sniff the rest of them back.

Without a word we both start walking again, and this time I go over to the cardboard box and pull open the flaps. "A block of cheese, some bread, two chocolate bars and a packet of custard creams," I say.

"Six cushions, covered in dog hair," says Noah.

"What colour?" I ask.

"Dog colour," he says, peering closely. "Sort of black and white. And grey – and brown."

I try to think of people with dogs. Everyone here has dogs. Did Sanjeev have a dog? Actually I don't think he likes dogs. I help myself to a custard cream, pinging the top layer off with my teeth and feeling the delicious sweetness coating my tongue. The best.

Noah goes to the back room and opens the door again. Offering him a custard cream, I join him to examine what's in there. Cardboard. There's a lot of cardboard. Most of it is from dog food boxes, some of it from those banana boxes from supermarkets. We haul it all out and Noah tries lying on a row of fruit boxes. "Not bad," he says, tugging a blanket around his shoulders and curling up his legs. "Can we just go to sleep and think about everything else in the morning? Pass that bread, I'll make myself a sandwich."

"You're going to go to sleep?" I say.

"Why not? There's nothing else happening."

"For god's sake, Noah. We should be trying to escape, not just lying down and sleeping."

"They're not going to do anything to us – they've just rescued us from a river. We're perfectly safe. When Uncle P pays the ransom we can go home."

"Just now they were pointing shotguns at us."

He sniffs and pulls the blanket up higher. "Turn the light out when you're done."

"Hang on," I say, remembering something I've just seen and swinging back into the tiny storeroom. There's a bag on the shelf, it's got the St David's logo on the side. I lug it down. It's heavy. "Is this yours?" I ask him.

Noah looks up. "No, I don't have one of those – only the rugby team have them."

"Odd," I say pulling it under the light and drawing the zip open. "What's all this…?" I pull out two neatly folded rugby shirts, two pairs of shorts, some socks and those things you put down your socks to stop your shins getting kicked. And then, underneath, a scrumpled receipt. "S. Gupta," I read out loud. "S. Gupta – that's Sanjeev."

"Who's Sanjeev? You mentioned him before."

"He's the teacher at St David's who went missing when you did. He teaches sport – rugby."

"Well, that would be why I don't know him – I managed to get out of rugby. Too dangerous, Mum said."

"But the shirts are stellar – here." I pass one to Noah. "Put it on. Just a sec while I change." I run back into the little room, peel off my wet shirt and pull on the rugby shirt, which is massive and dry and warm and hangs right down below my bum.

"Oh – thanks, Viv, that's lovely," says Noah, pulling the collar up and rubbing his arms. I push my feet into a pair of socks. I can feel every thread enveloping my cold toes. Delicious.

"But why's it here though?" I say, sitting back on the cardboard box and dragging a blanket over my legs. "I mean – why's Sanjeev Gupta's kit here? It means he must be connected. His disappearance must be connected." I stare at the floor. "But I just don't have him down as a kidnapper. And he always wore the strongest aftershave – I'd be able to smell him. Sniff this bag," I sniff it myself and pass it to Noah. "See? It really smells of manly sprinkly stuff."

"Dunno. Look, Viv – I'm so tired. Can I just go to sleep?"

Further inside the bag I find nothing more than some mints and a stopwatch so I turn the bag over, and that's when I see it.

"Oh, no – oh, god!" I say, staring at the black blotches across the underside of the bag.

"What?" says Noah, his eyes closed.

"You know when you bled all over the car, all over my bag? It looked exactly like this. It's blood. And lots of it."

Chapter 13

We lie, almost not frozen, in the dark, listening to the storm outside subside. The wind stops. Foxes bark. Something squeals, something calls – a duck? So we're still by the river then. Our little room is getting warmer. The cardboard makes a kind of mattress and with the dog cushions and the blankets we can be almost snuggly. Noah's breathing goes slow, nearing a snore, but I don't sleep. I can't sleep. I'm trying to work out what's going on with Sanjeev. If he was the kidnapper, he wouldn't have blood on his bag – not unless he'd killed someone, or Noah had had another nosebleed. And he hadn't. I asked him.

Which means the only other possibility is that the blood is Sanjeev's. That somehow, when Noah was being kidnapped, Sanjeev got involved. I think back to his kind face, lovely warm eyes. He's the kind of person who'd have a go. He'd probably try and grab a gun that was being pointed at someone.

"Wake up!" I say, bashing Noah's arm.

"What?" he says.

"When you were taken – grabbed. Where were you?"

"Don't you ever sleep? Why do you even want to know that?"

"I just do – tell me."

"If you have to know, I was behind the sports hall, on the way to the music block. I had my headphones on so I didn't hear anyone, and then there was a bag over my head and then I was in the back of a van – probably that van. That's it."

"And was there no one else around?"

There's a long silence and I wonder if he's gone back to sleep.

"Someone came out of the back door of the hall – I think."

"Who was it?"

"No one I know – a tall man. Probably one of them."

"Black hair?"

"Possibly – I don't know."

"He's very tall," I say. "And what about cars – were there any cars around?"

"Well, yes, it's a car park, *duh*..." he says.

"Yeah – OK."

I stare into the darkness above me and listen to the wind.

"Did you hear anything?"

"Oh, my god, Viv – are you going to let me sleep, or what?"

"Possibly," I say. "When I've worked it out. Do you think there's any chance that there was anyone else in the van with you?"

"What?"

"A body, say."

"Oh, god, that's horrible!"

"I know, but I can't come up with another reason for Sanjeev's bloodstained kit to be here. Unless he got caught up in it somehow and they ... well, they..."

"Killed him? To kidnap me?"

"They might not have done it on purpose – I

mean, it could have been accidental."

"Or it could be murder." I hear a long breath from Noah, like he's deflating. "Actually, Viv, there might have been someone else in the van with me. Someone groaned. I thought it was the driver, but it could have been a person. He might have been alive."

"What happened next?"

"We stopped, and they led me out of the van." He pauses. "No, hang on. There was a scuffle, some shouting – they were really angry. I fell down and for a second I didn't have anyone holding me. I got to my feet and started walking even though I had a bag over my head and my hands tied so I'd no idea where I was going."

"And?"

"They grabbed me and pushed me into a room, a shed – something with a wooden floor – and shut the door."

"Did you listen?"

Noah goes quiet for the longest time.

"I cried," he says in the end. "I couldn't hear much over that, but…"

"What?"

"I might have heard a shot."

"Oh!"

We lie in the dark, listening.

And something else occurs to me. I spring upright and switch on the light.

"What now?" he says, rubbing his eyes. "I need to sleep. I'm so tired."

"No, Noah – just no. Listen to me. They've got you because they want lots of money. You're worth money. But me – I'm an unplanned extra."

He blinks and stares at me, his brain processing the information.

"Just like Sanjeev must have been an unplanned extra. Except, of course, that his disappearance just helped them pin the crime on someone who was vaguely connected to you."

"What d'you mean?"

"That I need to get out of here, and well away from here. You, they need to keep safe. Me, they can..." The words get stuck in my throat. But I wanted to say, *kill*.

At that point, Noah does climb off his cardboard bed. We search the walls. We examine the door. The tiny window in the back room is ruled out as being too small. After a few minutes of hurried searching we're standing by the radiator, warming our hands.

"Where do you think we are?" asks Noah.

"I reckon we're upstream near the watercress beds. There's loads of empty countryside there – above the Blackwater Estate."

He nods.

I look back at Sanjeev's bag and shudder.

"Do you think they … shot him?" says Noah, reading my mind.

"What do you think?"

"There are other ways of bleeding," he says, sticking his finger up his nose and pulling down something that might be a leftover of his nose bleed.

"Yeah – but where is he? If it was Sanjeev, and he was in the van with you, and he was alive, and they didn't shoot him, where is he?" I get up and go into the back room again and look at the little window. It's got a plastic frame. Unhooking one of the shelf brackets, I pick at the plaster until it begins to come away and the corner of the window becomes clear. Outside, it's still dark, but it must be getting towards morning. Everyone will know I'm missing. Maria will have said. The waterkeepers should be looking for me. Even angry Lord B might start to try and find me. The thought makes me feel very slightly better. Only very slightly.

After ten minutes I've taken a few centimetres of plaster away, revealing some huge screws that seem to go through the window frame and into the wooden uprights of the shed.

"Ugh." I sit back on the toilet lid and sniff back a tear. "It's hopeless."

Noah's next door, still trying to work it out. "But if they did … *kill* him, where have they put the body?"

"I don't know, and just now, I don't care. We *have* to get out of here. Come on, please, think…" I scrub my knuckles against the side of my head as if my brain might work better that way.

"What about the roof? That's how we got out last time," he calls.

Through the doorway, I hear him clamber on to the freezer in the big room, and I do the same in the storeroom. The ceiling is polystyrene tiles, easily pushed aside, but beyond it, the roof is made of solid sheeting that I can't even begin to move. It doesn't seem to be attached in any way, it's seamless.

"That's not going to work," I hear from Noah, his voice disturbingly close. I look to my left and see his head sticking up into the roof space too.

"We could hide up here and jump down when they come again?" I say.

Noah thinks about it. "Nah. One of us might get out, but not two. And we don't even know what's outside."

He's right. We'd probably run a few metres before getting caught again. After making one more attempt at moving the sheet of whatever it is above my head, I give up and drop down to the storeroom floor. This is hopeless. There's nothing here. We can't flush ourselves down the drain, or float through the window. We can't call anyone.

Something, a random thought, nearly occurs to me but disappears the moment I try to pinpoint it, and then Noah shouts from next door. "Viv!" he calls. "What do you think about this?" Sticking my head round the doorframe, I see him buffeting the enormous freezer. "Momentum – or something," he says.

"Er – what exactly are you thinking?" I watch him struggling with the huge white box, rolling it back and forth on its tiny wheels, a centimetre or two with each shove.

"It's really heavy – right?"

"Yeah."

"We could use it as a battering ram – go straight through the side of the shed. It's only made of wood. What d'you think?" He straightens up, looking doubtful.

"Um," I say, thinking that this could be a complete waste of precious time. "We can try it."

"I knew you wouldn't like it. I don't know why I bother."

"I don't think it's an idiotic idea," I say. "It's just…"

"There's this too." He looks down at his foot. The metal collar has left a black ring around his ankle, and underneath that, a glowing, unhealthy redness. In the light, I can see that the collar is hinged and padlocked. "I think I' m stuck with it, aren't I?" he says.

Kneeling down, I pull it away from his calf. "There's quite a lot of room around it. Did you try and pull it off?"

"What do you think?" he replies. "Duh, I didn't just stand there waiting for you to come and rescue me."

"Stay there."

"I'm not going anywhere, am I?"

I go through to the storeroom and look around

for anything that might help. Big cardboard, small cardboard. Wood. a mug. Getting more and more frantic I tell myself that the water is not rising – that we are not going to drown. That I don't need to panic. But still I feel the fear taking over. We have to get out of here and soon. Perhaps we haven't got time to lose this ankle chain but we could run with it, bashing and clanging behind us.

No we can't. It has to come off. I start pulling things out of cupboards, cleaning polish, gun cotton, fish hooks. And then, behind the downpipe from the tiny basin next to the toilet – "Yes!" – a bottle of washing-up liquid, almost full, and pleasingly slimy.

"What are you going to do?" says Noah when I come back into the bigger room, holding my prize. "Wash it off?"

"Oh, shut up, Noah," I say, in a super-ordinary voice. Controlling my trembling hands, I squirt the green liquid all around the band and his foot. "Now, if I just hold this . . ." The green runs down his foot. ". . . and you pull – let's see."

Kneeling on the floor, I grip the metal ring, my fingers hooked over the top, and I guide it so that it wedges by Noah's heel. "If. . ." I wriggle the ring a little sideways and flakes of rust ping off and stick to his foot.

"Ow!" he says.

"Try pointing your toes, and pulling," I say. His heel is actually wedged part of the way through the ring, and I tug. Once. Twice.

"Ow!" he says again, and his foot comes free.

"Yay!" I say, as he rubs his ankle and a series of conflicting emotions cross his face. He still doesn't want to be grateful to me any more than I want to be grateful to him. "Now, let's get dressed."

Taking my jeans from the heater, I discover they have dry knees. That's the best I can say for them, but they're warmer than they were when I took them off. I've still got no shoes, but I do have Sanjeev's socks. For Noah's part, his trousers are wet, but we both have the rugby shirts and it has stopped raining.

I grab two plastic carrier bags and knot them over the socks, over the soles of my feet. Noah rips a hole in the middle of two blankets and makes us a couple of ponchos.

We each take a bite of cheese and cram several slices of bread in our mouths and the chocolate bars in our pockets.

I have a wee.

Noah has a wee.

We do all this calmly, trying not to panic. Trying not to listen out for the van returning, for the gates rattling. Trying not to just sit down and cry or scream or fall apart.

"Right," I say. "Freezer."

Chapter 14

Putting wheels on freezers might seem stupid, but when you think about it, how else are you supposed to move such enormous things? We unplug it.

We decide to go for the wall on the opposite side to the window. It might not be as solid and it will give us more time if they return while we're escaping because hopefully the hole we're about to make won't be visible from the van.

"Shall we empty it?" I ask peering inside. It's full of dead pheasants, all trussed up for the oven. I point at the neat rows of carcasses. "Connor?"

Noah raises an eyebrow. "He's got a gun. Plenty of guns. He runs the shoot. But I don't think anyone on the Blackwater Estate would…"

We leave the pheasants in the ice. We need the freezer heavy if this is going to work.

Pointing it at the chosen spot on the wall we shove as hard as we can. By the time it hits the plaster, it's motoring, and it makes a huge dent.

Slowly, we pull it to the opposite side of the room and get it rolling fast across the floor.

Thump

This time it smashes through the plaster and takes out a small wooden prop from the inside of the wall.

"Excellent," says Noah.

The third time we charge, the freezer punctures the outside wall, and we discover that the shed is clad in wood.

The fourth time, it loosens a vertical prop – and together we work the prop back and forth until it gives up and comes away in our hands.

The fifth time, the freezer smashes through the wall and keeps going until it vanishes, leaving a waist-high doorway.

We stare.

"Wow!" I say.

"Wow!" Noah says.

Tiptoeing in my plastic-bag shoes I step through the wall of the shed and stop, sharp.

"How did we not know this was here?" I say.

"Water. More water?"

Lit by a huge moon in a clear sky is what appears to be a lake. On its side in the lake is our freezer, bouncing lightly as the frozen pheasants leave and water enters.

I turn to look at the shed. It is a shed. A lone building in a compound by a lake. It's utterly unfamiliar, and yet we can't be very far from home. There's about a metre of land before the water begins, which must usually be a patch of grass, and huge chain-link fences that stretch out into the water on either side, and would presumably normally just be on land. We're caught in a half moon of ground trapped between the water and the fence. Skirting around the shed we examine the metal gates, which are two metres high and locked.

"I might be able to get over that," Noah says, grasping the chain-link and pulling himself upward. I watch as he does. I don't think I could get over it. I'm short and it's tall. But I don't say anything –

and feel selfishly relieved when he fails and drops back to the ground. We pace the fence, looking for an imaginary hole or imaginary wire cutters. It just ends in the lake in both directions.

"This is..." He sighs and kicks the wall of the shed.

Swallowing a growing lump of fear, I stomp around, checking to see if there's anything we could use to get away, when I have a sudden thought.

"The freezer – it's obvious!"

* * *

It takes a while to empty it. There must be a hundred pheasants inside, and we have to use the washing-up liquid bottle to get the water out of the bottom. And we can't really see anything. And then we have the problem of the door.

"We've got to take it off or we'll tip up."

"But it won't come off! Oh, this is ridiculous!" Noah says sitting back on the shore. "Hopeless – let's just give up, wait for them to come back. Uncle P will pay, you know. We're not going to die."

"No," I say, thinking of the bloodstained bag. "No, that's so not true! We really might die. Or I might. We've got to make this work." In the moonlight I find the screw heads and, using my thumbnail, make a fumbling attempt to undo them.

All I do is break my thumbnail.

"What do we need?" sighs Noah, standing and turning back towards the shed.

"A penny – a thin metal thing? Anything flat and narrow."

I drag the freezer towards the shore so that the light from the torn hole in the shed falls on to the screw holes and Noah reappears and hands me a fishhook.

"What?" I say, looking at the tiny thing in my hand.

"They're very strong. Just watch out for the barb bit."

He tries one end of the lid and I try the other. Finally, just as I'm giving up hope, one of the screws gives in and begins to turn.

"It's working!" I shout, my voice horribly loud and bouncing across the water.

It takes an age, all the time the moon's tracking back over the sky and I know the morning's going to come soon and with the morning, surely they'll be back.

Ping.

The last screw falls inside the box.

"Paddles," says Noah and he races back to rip something off the outside of the building.

Together we right the freezer and push it into the water and although it's heavy, there comes a moment when the water takes the weight. I test it by bouncing my hand on the side and it seems to be relatively stable.

"It floats!" he says.

"Yeah," I say, running back through the hole and grabbing the last blankets, and turning off the light.

"What are you doing?" asks Noah.

"Buying us time." Wading through the water with my bag-covered feet, I clamber in and crouch in the bottom. "Try getting in," I say.

"Why are you down there?" he says, looking over the side.

"So it doesn't tip up," I mumble. The freezer smells of old freezer smells, stale bread and rotting things. Noah stumbles in behind me, and we both try kneeling up a little.

Our rectangular boat bumps on the bottom of the lake, but when Noah pushes down against the ground with a piece of wood, we bounce off and drift very slightly away from the shore. I watch the moon spin slowly from right to left and realise that we must be caught in a stream.

"I don't think it's a lake," I say.

Kneeling up, Noah sticks his head over the side, making the whole thing rock scarily.

"How far from the shed have we got?"

"It's getting smaller," he says.

I risk looking over the side. The shed is getting smaller, but we're right in the middle of the water in a white box, moonlit. If they appear any time soon, we'll be caught.

Just as I'm thinking this, headlights swing through the trees over by the shed, and I hear an engine.

Oh, no.

"Paddle," I say.

Both of us kneel up and as quickly and silently as possible, we dip and push, dip and push, using the boards that Noah tore from the shed to get the freezer gliding through the water. Except that it doesn't really glide, it sort of waddles, and I'm guessing that because it's not boat-shaped, we're not going to move as well or as fast as we could.

The metal gates clank behind us. The engine roars and the van stops by the shed, which is now backlit by the headlights.

With my plank in my hand I dig deep into the water, pushing forward, listening, while looking backwards.

Bolts rattle, which must be on the outside of the door, and then a light appears in the ragged hole in the side of the shed.

"What?" A voice bounces over the still surface of the water.

"Quick, hang the blankets over the sides," I whisper, and fumbling our planks back into the bottom of our boat, we dangle the dark blankets over the shiny white sides. There's just one quarter that's not covered and I pray that we won't drift round. Barely breathing, we hide back in the bottom of the freezer.

"Where the hell...?" says a voice. A local voice.

Then there's the low rumble of two people talking and then I hear the crisp sound of feet on the tiny shoreline.

Someone yanks at a plank, the nail squeaks and they throw it in the water.

More voices, and thumps, and then wet sounds as someone wades in and pulls something out of the water. The door, they've found the freezer door.

Seconds later, feet sound, running on the shore, and then a torch beam plays over the lake, catching the trees on the other side.

"Oh, god," mutters Noah.

Squishing into the bottom of our boat, I listen, trying to recognise the voices, using that as a way to stop myself panicking. But my mind's already halfway to panic. Is it better to sit up and paddle – or lie down and pretend to be dead? If I die here, will I sink? Will anyone ever know what happened to us? Will the police think Mum and I were in league, that we kidnapped Noah; that I tried to take him away from rescuers in a chest freezer with no shoes on?

Stars pass over the rectangular patch of sky above us.

We're drifting away – but just not fast enough. They might even be able to wade out to us. And then we twist, Orion and the moon revolve, the freezer swings a whole three hundred and sixty degree turn.

"Hey!" goes a voice on the shore.

Bang.

Sleeping ducks take off, squawking, and something patters on the surface of the water.

"Shotgun pellets," whispers Noah.

Of course.

The next shot sprays the side of the freezer with something that sounds like hail, and the last of the ducks take off.

Then there's a pause, and the freezer swings back, and I'm kind of aware that we're moving faster because the moon disappears completely.

Bang.

The pellets hit hard and fast, one of them bouncing from the outside and tumbling into the freezer.

Bang.

Again, it's a direct hit. *Are they trying to sink us?*

"Paddle," says Noah. He springs up, and I spring up alongside him and we risk three dips each while the distant sound of someone reloading a shotgun in the dark drifts over the water.

"Down!" he shouts.

Bang.

They don't let off the second shot, and we wait. Our tiny moment of paddling has moved us further into the stream and the sounds change. From the expanse of open water, we move to something narrower – there's trickling water somewhere close, and when I look up I can see trees behind us.

Bang.

This time, no pellets hit us, and the voices are definitely distant.

So slowly I can practically hear my bones move, I sit up and look over the side.

"We're in the river," I say.

Noah sits up beside me.

There's the faintest suggestion of pink in the sky behind the bony trees. And it reflects on the black water. Mist begins to rise all around us, and with the light comes the realisation of where we are.

Just above the Blackwater Estate.

Chapter 15

"If we paddle, we could be home by breakfast," says Noah, sitting up and rocking the freezer so much that a small wave crests over the side.

"Sit down! You'll tip us into the river."

Now we're in the river proper, our "boat" is demonstrating why boats aren't freezer-shaped. With every new current, it twists around, and more and more and more water seems to be coming in.

"I think we've got a leak," says Noah, energised, his halo of blond hair catching in the dawn light. "Yeah – here, look!"

He's pointing to a small hole in the end of the

tank. And I see that it's next to another small hole. In fact, there are masses of them, and they're all letting in water.

"It's where the shotgun pellets hit us," he says, flattening his hands against them as if that's going to make enough of a difference. "They were definitely trying to sink us. And it's working."

Ahead of us is a bridge. It's the lane that crosses the tip of the estate – once we're underneath it we'll be in the estate again. The kidnappers will know that – and under normal circumstances they'd be on the bridge waiting for us, but everything's changed. The whole landscape is under water. As the light comes up and the shadows recede, the effect of the rain becomes clear. The bridge, which should have a lane crossing it, stands alone in a lake anchored by the white railing that marks the road. The arches have disappeared under the water level, so that when we reach it, we just bump up against the side.

"Now what?" asks Noah.

"I think we should get out and walk along the lane," I say.

"But then they'll get us – that's mad."

"If we send our friend Freezer on his way

downstream, they'll think we're still in it."

"Like a decoy?" he says. "That'll never work. We should paddle to the side and get out in the woods."

I don't bother to answer, and using my hands flat on the bricks walk the freezer along to the end of the actual brick bridge until it grates on the lane. I leap out, gasping as the freezing cold water reaches my armpits, bracing myself against the flow. "Get out! Hurry, we don't know how long it'll take for them to get here," I shout, wading through the water.

"You're mad," he says, slinging one leg over the side.

"I'm right," I say, pulling at the side of the freezer, feeling the wheels grip on the bridge. "We just need to..." The force of the water easily pushes the thing over the tarmac and shoots it out the other side, bouncing on the water and whirling away downstream.

I watch it for about a second before struggling over the bridge, keeping the rail in my hand until the water level drops below my knees and I begin to feel as if I'm not going to be swept away.

Behind me, Noah sloshes through the water,

grumbling and mumbling, and I feel all my anger from yesterday seeping back.

I try to run through the shallows and he doesn't so the gap becomes bigger and that just makes me crosser. That brief time last night when we bonded again seems to have slipped away with the floodwater. He's Noah Belcombe, and I'm me. Polar opposites.

Am I jealous? I think about his entitlement, his rights, and yes, I am – but it's not that I want to be him. He's an old-fashioned mistake. I just want people like him, and his "generous" family, not to *be*. Full stop.

I realise that what I want is equality – I don't want us all to go around having to bow to Lord and Lady B. I don't want Mum to wipe the mud from their boots, or the blood from Noah's face. I don't want them to be first class and us second.

Right now though, Noah has shoes and I have plastic bags. That just about sums it up.

Ahead of us the road emerges from the water. The Blackwater Estate is on our right, the woodland on our left, and behind us I hear the distant revving of an engine. It might be coincidence or it might be the kidnappers at the edge of the flood on the other side of the river.

I don't know how far a shotgun can fire, but I don't want to find out.

"Hurry up," I say, splashing through the last few metres of the flood, but Noah's heard the engine too and he's finally moving at a decent pace.

Unwelcoming woods rear up before us, bordered by a ditch full of water and brambles, and then a blackthorn thicket.

"We can't go in there," shouts Noah, racing past me along the lane. "Keep going."

I try to speed up, but I'm so slow. It's as if my limbs have filled with ice, heavy ice, and I waste more time looking back towards the bridge.

I can't see the men, but I can see the freezer, bobbing on downstream. A moment later, the engine sounds again and there's a crunch of gears and revving, and whatever it is they came in turns and goes the other way.

"S'all right." My legs stop dead and I pant, leaning over, propping my hands on my knees to draw breath.

As I straighten up, a little feeble sunlight warms up the road, and mist rises from everywhere – the water, the land, Noah himself.

A rabbit pops out on to the lane, sees us and leaps back into the hedge.

For a moment, everything feels really normal. Even standing in a pair of dead man's socks on the side of the road.

"The sawmill," says Noah, sinking to his haunches. "It opens at eight. It must be nearly eight."

He's right. Dave runs the sawmill. He's OK – he's a safe place to run to.

Exhausted, we climb over a stile into a field of thistles. My plastic-bag shoes have almost completely disappeared, leaving knotted plastic around my ankles and Sanjeev's socks, and it takes me ages to pick my way across.

"Come on, loser," says Noah.

So we've both gone from love to hate.

Perhaps that makes it easier – we can say whatever we like.

"I'm not the loser. If I hadn't been out there, you'd have drowned in that shed."

"They'd have rescued me; I'm too valuable," he says.

"That. *That's* your problem," I say, stopping to pick a thorn out of my foot. "You think you're too precious to deal with the rest of us. Too … special. Too privileged. Don't you? Eh?"

"Shut up, Viv," he says. "I'm too tired for this rubbish. I know you're the salt of the earth and I'm a good-for-nothing toff, but we're stuck in this together."

I do shut up. I'm too tired as well. Images of bed and duvets and warm feet flicker before me as I avoid the final few thistles and make it to the hedge. Awkwardly, we pick our way through a strand of barbed wire and a hawthorn bush and I'm forced to help Noah by holding the wire away from his golden tresses.

"Rapunzel," I say.

"What?"

"Nothing."

In silence we trek over another field where the river is lapping at the side, the fence posts sticking out of the water like a pier.

Bright fury fizzles down to a slow-burning ember about halfway across.

We cross a track, and pause by the huge yew tree where Daisy and I used to sit when we were little. Its roots cover the bank, dry and dusty already as if it's drunk every drop of water the flood could produce. Red sap clots on the trunk and I wonder if we could hole up here for a few hours and sleep, but Noah and his shoes march on.

Limping, my bare feet follow. I remember his sneer when he saw me with my Herschel High friends at the bus stop last week as he went past in the St David's minibus. Why did I bother to rescue him? And I think of all the names that I've ever wanted to call him. *Tadpole, Inbred, Slug,* and now I invent some more.

I think about all the least lovely things on the planet and I say them out loud. "Cockroach, scorpion, puffer fish, what are those things that lie under the sand...?"

"Weaver fish," he says.

"Oh, yes, weaver fish, pterodactyl, Komodo dragon, Japanese knotweed..."

"What are you doing?" he asks.

"Thinking of horrible things," I say.

"Mouldy cheese, school suet puddings, cough mixture, Grandma's creosote cough mixture in particular. Woollen rugby socks, woollen rugby shorts, rugby, Latin, Mr Dexter the French teacher, gym, being shot at... Why?"

"Oh – nothing," I say. I realise I have no experience

of learning Latin, or woollen rugby shorts – or even school suet puddings. The life that he lives and the life that I live are so totally different.

"There," he says, stopping. "The sawmill at last."

And we both let out a long sigh of relief.

Chapter 16

As we enter the yard, Dave rumbles down the track in his pickup and screeches to a halt. "Noah! Viv!" he calls, throwing the door open and stumbling over to us, his engine still running. "What the—"

"Dave!" shouts Noah, breaking into a shambolic trot. "Dave! Take me home." He holds his arms out as if he's waiting for a hug.

But Dave shies away from Noah and laughs awkwardly. "I think I'd better call the police. Come inside, get dry – what are you wearing? I've got some biscuits. I'll check the state of the milk – should be able to make tea."

We follow him as he unlocks the doors and ushers us inside the massive building. The mill is warm – there's a wood burner slumbering in the corner of the boxed-off plywood office and we rush towards it, holding our frozen hands out in front of us.

"Oh – sweet!" I say. "Thank you." Without making eye contact, Dave puts the kettle on. Chucking a load of kindling on the fire he makes the flames leap and the heat doubles. He seems nervous, but then I suppose he's not very used to people. Normally he's here on his own, I don't suppose anyone comes into this office much. He certainly never let us in here when we were younger.

As we press ourselves as near to the stove as we dare, Dave gets out his phone and wanders out of the office. "Just going to ring the police," he says, and fumbles with the phone, his big fingers uncomfortable with the screen. It slips out of his hand into a pile of sweepings and he kneels down and picks it up, wiping off the sawdust.

Noah doesn't say anything. He keeps his hands about a millimetre from the hot cast iron and starts to shake, a little at first and then great juddering shudders that course through him. I wonder if it's just the cold, or is it shock too?

He's looking at his quaking arms as if they belong to someone else.

Next door, Dave's speaking to someone on his mobile. I can see him through the little window. He finishes the call and then rings someone else. I catch a bit of the conversation: "Yes, both of them," he says, but he doesn't sound happy.

Which is odd.

Putting his phone back in his pocket he wanders back in and sees Noah clamping his hands under his armpits to stop the shuddering.

"Better have a hot drink." Dave clatters about with the kettle. "Tea all right?"

"Yes," I answer.

While teabags steep in cups, Dave posts some more wood shavings into the fire and the little glass screen turns from yellow to white hot. My jeans begin to steam. Underneath, my legs begin to scorch, but I don't care, I'm so bone cold. Lifting the rugby shirt, I let the heat scald my T-shirt until my frozen stomach turns pink. I peel one of Sanjeev's socks off my feet and examine the holes in my toes that the thistles made.

Two mugs of caramel-coloured tea arrive in

front of us along with a packet of custard creams.

I hold up a custard cream. "Custard creams keep on happening," I say, mostly to myself.

"We're free," says Noah after a few minutes. "We made it, Viv."

"Yes," I say. "We did." But somehow this doesn't feel like I think it ought to. Where's the euphoria? I should feel overjoyed, overwhelmed by sudden freedom. For some reason I just feel really nervous. Maybe that's because we've already been rescued once. Or not.

"They'll be here soon," says Dave. "Get that tea down you." And then, in un-Dave-like chattiness, he asks, "So – Noah – who dunnit then? Who took you? Any ideas?"

Noah sips his tea; his hand is still shaking. "No," he says. "I never saw them."

"You?" Dave asks me, opening his gun cabinet and popping some shotgun cartridges back into a box. Everyone here has guns, I realise. The estate's full of them.

"No," I say. "I didn't either." Dave's hands are shaking as badly as Noah's.

"S'pect the police'll ask you – did you get the voices or nothing? You know, recognise anything?"

There's something awkward in his questions.

I slurp my tea and leave it up to Noah to speak. Everything is making me more uncomfortable. Every tic of Dave's face, every biscuit, every blackbird song outside. I eat two more biscuits and drink the tea while it's still too hot.

"There was nothing I recognised," says Noah, staring into the fire. And then, "When d'you think the police'll get here?"

Dave considers the question. "Take 'em a while – the river's up, you see. Can't cross Elbow Bridge, the weed rack over at Cobber's Wood's gone under, the ford's armpit-deep at Easton – so they'll have to drive all the way round. Half an hour, I reckon. Unless they got a helicopter."

"Oh." Noah pokes his finger in his tea to remove a dead fly. "OK. Could I ring my mum?"

"I rung your mum," says Dave. "She's coming over directly."

"That's good," says Noah, looking more cheerful.

Probably another minute passes while I turn around and let the bum of my jeans toast and feel the cold on the front of my legs, and I begin to wonder if the sawmill has a toilet.

Then a vehicle pulls into the yard. I glance out

of the window; I'm expecting the police, or Lady B, but it isn't – it's a van.

Dave doesn't seem to notice. "Come and have a look around – you haven't been here for years, you two, have you? You used to play in here, didn't you, Viv? Nothing but trouble I seem to remember."

"Dave – who's that?" I say.

"Dunno," he says, looking where I've been looking. "Someone for wood, I reckon. Or a courier – ordered a couple of bandsaw blades a day or so ago." Dave shuffles out of the office and towards the big doors at the entrance. "I'll just be a tick – stay here in the warm."

I don't. Of course I don't. I never do anything I'm told, which is why the first thing that I notice about the man that's getting out of the van is a ski mask. The second, something that could be a shotgun.

Oh, no.

"Noah – this isn't good," I say.

"What?" he asks. "We're safe aren't we?"

"Let's get out of here."

"Uh?" says Noah, frowning.

"The van – it's them!"

I drag him out of the office and into the middle

of the sawmill. There's no way out except for the main doors. Unless ... above us is the long rail that runs the length of the room. From it hang loops of cable, like huge curtain rings. They're supposed to allow a person to move wood the length of the building without using the forklift truck. When we were little, Daisy and I tried to use it as a zip wire. We pretended that it was how Hansel and Gretel got out of the gingerbread house – that the little window at the end was the only way out, and that the main entrance was the oven. If you got it completely right, you could shoot through the window at the end. If you got it wrong, you hit the wall. Either way, Dave used to shout at us.

I point up. "We gotta go."

Noah heaves a heavy sigh. "Or what?"

"Them," I say. Feet sound on the gravel outside. "Tell you later," I shout, jumping for the cable, hooking my foot into the loop and shoving myself along the length of the rail, punting along the huge shelves of planked wood lining the sides until I'm moving fast towards the little window at the end.

Noah clatters behind me, his loop crashing into mine, and we jerk our way to the far end.

Behind us, the entrance doors scrape open.

"Hey!" shouts Dave. "Hey!"

"Window – mine," yells Noah, and he leaps, landing on the tiny plank windowsill and throwing himself forward through the gap until, still flying with the momentum of the zip wire, he drops from view.

Shoving against the piles of wood on either side, I reach for the exit. Why is Noah faster than me? Five metres, four, three...

Something hits the ceiling of the sawmill, bringing down a million cobwebs and a ton of dust and just missing my flailing legs.

A net?

I make it to the windowsill and drop towards the ground as a short length of wood whizzes past me. Freefalling, I plummet but land in mud that's soft with rain and lorry tyres and blissfully empty of men in ski masks throwing things.

Slightly winded, I stagger towards Noah, who's already trying to get through the fence, but once again his hair's got caught in the wire.

"Here, stop," I yell, and yank his hair out of the barbs.

"Ow! Viv!" he squawks, and I throw myself through the gap too.

A dog begins to bark and the throwing intensifies. Missiles fall all around us – some of them making contact. "Ow!" yells Noah, rubbing his thigh.

The ground's so squidgy we're almost wading as we run up the slight hill behind the sawmill, not daring to look back.

"Did they…?" pants Noah. "What was that?"

"I don't know," I mumble, trying to get past him, trying to get him between me and whoever it is who's throwing stuff.

We stumble and lurch and nearly make it over the top of the hill before a large chunk of wood bounces right by my foot and knocks me sideways.

More spars thud into the turf behind us and an engine roars, tyres whining on the mud at the bottom of the hill – and I suddenly find I can run faster than I ever could before.

Alongside me, Noah's gasping and he too seems to have discovered sprinting. We race over the top of the slope and down the other side into a thick belt of river mist where we slow down to a fast run. I know that off to our left, over two fields, is the group of trees that marks the quarry.

"Run for quarry," I say. "We need to head that way."

"House," he coughs.

"Can't get over the river."

"But quarry?" Proper sentences are too much effort.

"Cos beyond it, we can get to Blackwater Abbas. There's the village shop. We need to get off the estate."

"What?"

"We do – we need to get clear of here."

"I don't know," pants Noah. "I just know I've gotta slow down."

"Slow down and we die. We have to get off the estate." The words come out as a cough, and I keep on running, one foot in front of the other – one bare foot, one socked foot.

My mind's playing over what just happened. What I think just happened.

"They were the kidnappers – who broke into the sawmill?" asks Noah.

"Don't think they broke in," I say, thinking.

"What?" he stumbles alongside me, both of us still just about running.

"Something happened there," I say, working it all out.

Now the immediate panic's over, I can feel my

bare foot on the frozen ground. It's bruised and sore and red, and my socked foot's not doing much better. My feet really want all this to stop.

Finally he asks the question that's been going round and round my brain. "So are you saying that Dave is part of it?"

We jog about another fifty metres before I answer. "I … I dunno. Yes – almost certainly," I say. "I heard him shout – like he was arguing with someone, and the missiles were wild. He might have stopped someone actually firing *at* us. And he was so nervous, dropping things." I take a dozen deep breaths. "Not sure, but he definitely knows something."

The mist swirls around us, thicker and thicker, making it barely possible to see the ground. Distantly, a vehicle grinds a gear. A duck lands on the water.

"I hope you're wrong," says Noah after a while.

Chapter 17

A line of trees rise out of the mist in front of us, their branches bare and cold.

"You sure that's the quarry?"

"Yeah," I say, stumbling over frozen earth rather than icy grass.

"But you haven't been here for years; you can't be sure."

"I came a few days ago – to look for you."

"Did you?" He stops, leaning over and putting his hands on his knees, sucking in lungfuls of air. "Really?"

A crow calls in the distance.

"I did," I say, stopping alongside him. "With Chris. At the beginning, we thought you were hiding. Well, I did. I thought you were teaching your parents some kind of lesson – you know, heavy-duty sulking."

"Oh." He walks on, but I can see that his shoulders have lifted. I've evidently told him something that's made him feel good.

The field runs out and we trace a hedge until we can find a way through. It's prickly and this time I get caught on a thorn. Noah unpicks my collar from the bramble and we stumble down the slope until we can see the quarry below us.

It looks very quiet.

"They won't think we'd come here," he says in the end.

"Maybe not."

"Dave doesn't know anything about us; he's got no idea where we'd go."

"Depends who the others are."

I wish I hadn't said that. We shuffle in silence through the mist, sunlight high above us lighting the red of the beeches and releasing leaves in a slow stream that drifts down and settles somewhere under the whiteness. All I can imagine now is that someone is hunting us – and I'm thinking of Sanjeev and everything feels horrible.

Brambles catch at my knees and I stop. It might not actually be possible for me to get down to the quarry itself, but we need to cross it to get out towards the village. It's either that or a whole load of fields with no easy path. This is so much faster but I'd forgotten how scrubby the ground is and with no shoes on my feet it feels silly to walk over it. I squeeze myself past a burdock bush, but a mass of burrs catch on the rugby shirt, just adding to the misery. Each time I move, I pick up more.

Noah stamps ahead and I hear him open the car door. It creaks and then I hear him yelp.

"Tigger! You idiot!" And then, "You dozy cat, what are you doing here?"

It takes me an age to pick my way through the brambles and I fail to avoid some lightly crushed nettles that spring up to brush against my ankles. "Ow!"

Tigger yowls and pads towards me as if I might produce a bowl of cat food. The sight of him, so familiar, so warm and ordinary – I have to blink back tears.

I pick him up and hold him to my neck, avoiding

the burrs, great warm cat that he is, and he purrs and almost feels as if he might hug me back before he breaks away and leaps to the roof of the old car.

"Shame you didn't leave anything to eat here," says Noah, checking the mouldy interior.

I decide to ignore him.

"We need to go that way." I point off towards another branch of the river that circles the back of the quarry.

"Yeah," says Noah, and as if he's forgotten that we're being pursued by someone, several people, possibly with shotguns, he shuffles about, poking his head into the back of the car and sniffing.

I look down at my feet. They're so grubby it's hard to tell how damaged they are – but now they're fizzing from the stinging nettles and I'm pretty sure there's a thorn in my heel and the cold's penetrated so deep I'm not sure it'll ever leave. Lifting my left foot, I try massaging it. It's numb and in my hand it feels as if it belongs to a dead person. "I'll just inspect them," I say, sitting back against the bonnet. Tigger pads down the windscreen and pushes at my back, and then quite suddenly stops. His legs bend into a crouch and his huge yellow eyes scan the hedgerow.

"What is it, Tigger?" I whisper, putting my hand out to touch Noah's sleeve.

All three of us stop. We stop everything, especially breathing.

The mist is milky and thick outside the boundary of the quarry. Inside, it's grainy, like someone rubbed the air with ash. It means that everything is slightly colourless, slightly fuzzy.

I scan the bushes that make up the ring that surrounds us but I can't see anything. Tigger might just have spotted a big mouse, but he's sniffing the air now like there's an enemy out there.

And then he leaps – and an angry dog bursts through the gap at the end of the quarry – and we run. All four of us, Tigger well in front, the dog snapping behind us.

There's no way I can do anything about my feet and I pound over thistles, brambles and frost to get clear.

Tigger vanishes into a tree.

"I can't climb that," shouts Noah, a pace behind me.

"No," I yell. "Left – go left."

A stream with burst banks curls in from our right and we race over a plank bridge and wade through waterlogged grass, ice shells cracking around our feet but the water's nothing to the dog and it piles on behind us, snapping at Noah.

"Ow!" yells Noah. "It bit me."

Tall burdock plants laden with prickly fruit bend over the water, their stems thin and bent. I grab two, yanking them out of the soil and turn, holding them towards the dog who snaps and barks and growls – but he stops, watching my hand.

"What are you doing? Run," mutters Noah, who's backing away towards a stile in the next hedge, clutching his hand.

I jab at the dog. It steps backwards and then lunges around the burdock towards me, but I swipe sideways, cracking the burrs on the dog's nose.

"Yow!" The dog recoils, whining as the burrs glue themselves across his muzzle. He tries to come forward again, but I lash out with the other branch and this time they fix themselves all over his forehead like a painful crown.

"Go away," I shout as he tries to swipe them off with a paw. But the burrs won't be swiped, and spread themselves up his legs. Thrown by this sudden inconvenience he seems to forget about us, and I step over the stile, leaving the branches still laden with burrs across the wood as a barrier. For a second it looks as if the dog might follow, then he stops, listens to the air for a moment and trots away.

"Let's see your hand," I say, turning to Noah.

Pulling up the sleeve of the rugby top he shows me a neat set of four punctures, not bleeding heavily, but bleeding all the same.

"Does it hurt a lot?" I ask.

Noah nods and pinches his lips together. I can see tears welling in his eyes.

"I don't really know what to do about it," I say. "I think you should probably try and keep it clean."

"Rabies," he says.

"I doubt it," I say. "I think bats are more dangerous for that. But we'll get it seen to as soon as we can."

We jog over the field. With every step, my feet protest.

"Have you ever seen that dog before?" he pants.

"Looked a bit like Chris Mumford's dog, Lady." I catch a tussock with my foot and stumble, nearly falling full length. "But I don't think it can be – she's always on Chris's heel. She's really well trained. She's lighter than that too."

We stagger into the next field, this one pocked with cow footprints, and run on. Legs burning, lungs burning, feet burning.

"Chris's got two dogs – Lady and another one that looks like Lady. Can't remember what it's called," Noah pants. "He keeps it off the estate."

We run on.

"But that dog was angry," he says. "Can't possibly be Chris's – must be a stray."

"Oh," I say, and another distant thought begins to form in my mind, and it's not happy.

* * *

Mid-morning, the rain comes again. It's as if someone's emptying a bucket over our heads and we get soaked in seconds. "This is illogical," says Noah, stopping and leaning on a fence post. "We're so close to home – we should be trying to get there." He's holding his arm as if it really hurts and I can see that his fingers are starting to swell.

"Like how?" I say, watching drips falling from his ringlets, and feeling something between irritation and pity. "You thinking of swimming?"

"I don't know, we could demand a tractor from a farm or something."

"You might be able to demand a tractor – d'you

think anyone would lend me one?" I point at the tattered plastic-bag ringlets around my feet, the enormous rugby top that reaches my knees and my filthy jeans. "Anyway, there isn't a farm. The farm's on the other side of the river. Everything's on the other side of the river."

"Except the kidnappers," he says. "And a dog with large teeth."

I look beyond him. We're probably outside the Blackwater Estate by now. I don't think I've ever been this far over, and I can't work out where the river is in relation to the village. Floodwater's changed the landscape so much I probably couldn't point out where home is.

"I might just fall asleep here," he says. "You can tell them I died of wet."

Looking at him properly, I see that he's horribly pale. Some of it's the colour of his skin, and some of it is the rain on his hair. A medusa assortment of rat-tailed ringlets frame his face and he's shaking again. I'm not shaking, but that could just be because I've gone beyond it.

It could be an infection from the dog bite.

"Come on, Noah – one foot in front of the other," I say. "We'll be there soon."

He trails behind me, slower and slower. Hours and hours pass. Stumbling and mumbling we wander, possibly in circles.

"It's the Blackwater Bonfire tonight," I say eventually. "There'll be fireworks everywhere," I add, noting that the rain is getting heavier by the minute.

"Oh," he says, barely walking now.

The rain beats down around us, bouncing on the fallen leaves, all the orange of the morning turning into grey afternoon.

"What's the worst that could happen?" he asks in the end.

"We die of exposure?" I say, not mentioning the dog bite.

"No, I mean if they catch us?"

I think about it for a moment.

"They could recapture you – and I suppose get the ransom for you. I just don't know what they'd do with me."

"But you've never seen them – you don't know who they are. You're not a risk to them, are you?"

"I know Dave's involved, somehow," I say, thinking of all the things circling in my mind, some of which are making me feel really uncomfortable.

"And I think maybe someone else from the estate. And there's something that's been bothering me. When they picked us out of the river, they never asked me for my phone – they never checked that I didn't have one."

"You were sopping wet. Your phone would be flooded."

"Some phones are waterproof."

We wade through another boggy patch of grass.

"What are you saying?"

"It's as if they knew I didn't have my phone. Like they knew me – personally. They knew my phone was taken by the police."

"Oh," he says, but I'm not sure he understands.

"That's why we're heading for the village. To get off the estate."

"I think you're wrong. So what if Dave is involved – he's not a bad man. I'm sure he'll regret anything that's happened," he says. "My parents can pay the ransom – and we'll be free."

Is he being deliberately obtuse? "What about Sanjeev? What about the person groaning in the back of the van? The bloodstains in the bag? The missing body?" I find myself shouting. "Go on then," I say, trying to control my fear, my anger.

"Go and find them – go and walk up to them with their gun and their dog and their manacles. Go on!"

Noah turns and takes a couple of paces back the way we came.

"Go on!"

"Viv, come with me. I'm scared."

"I'm scared too – that's why I'm walking the other way."

"Viv – please."

"No way," I say. "No way. I'm going to find my way to somewhere I can call the police myself. I'm going to walk out of here. I'm going to… Oh, I don't know, I'm just going to survive." Stumbling away over the waterlogged grass, I pick my way between blackthorn bushes until I reach a gate that gives on to yet another field, this time full of wet sheep.

"Viv!" Noah calls. "Viv!"

Although I want to, I don't look round. Instead, I clamber over the gate, my feet leaden and dead on the bars, and drop heavily into the sheep field. The animals scatter away from me, and then wander closer, peering curiously at this strange half-human creature.

"Hello, sheep," I say, looking out for another

gate. In the far hedge is a gap. I waddle towards it, my feet so painful I can hardly bear to put them down on the cropped grass. The rain picks up, and now there's nothing remotely dry about anything. Water drips down my neck, my chest, through the gaps in my fists.

"Viv." But I won't turn.

"Viv." Again.

The gap seems to take an age to get to – and when I finally reach it, it turns out to be a gate and it's almost dark. A vehicle trundles along a lane a couple of fields over and the two cones of its headlights light up the rain racing through the sky.

Risking a look behind me, I see a shape approaching through the sheep. Noah.

Part of me wants to punch him. Part of me's glad he's changed his mind.

By the time he catches up with me, the sky's got an orange streak across the bottom, below the heavy clouds, and the temperature's dropping.

"OK," he says, cradling his hand in his other arm. "Where are we going?"

Chapter 18

It's dark, and we can't see what we're doing, and Noah may or may not be developing rabies or an infection or turning into a werewolf. But there's nowhere warm to hide, or to stop, and I think we're both aware that if we don't keep moving we'll die of cold. The cup of tea and the biscuit at the sawmill are such distant memories I'm beginning to think they weren't real. I'm also beginning to wonder about the dog.

That dog was like Lady, but it wasn't Lady.

And if Chris has another dog…

What was it doing there? Did it follow us all the

way from the sawmill?

Was Chris at the sawmill?

I can believe it of Dave – but Chris? No. Surely not.

I stumble in front and Noah stumbles behind. Brambles catch on my clothes, hook my skin, but I don't care any more. And my feet. My feet are on fire.

On the plus side it hasn't rained for at least an hour.

"Why isn't there a village? Or a house?" says Noah at last.

I don't bother to answer; I think it's a rhetorical question.

He's right though. The blackness seems to extend in every direction. Sometimes, a distant pair of headlights catch skeletal branches, and for a second I know which way to go, but mostly, it's just dark.

"No lights, no people, no kidnappers," he says.

"Hmm," I say, and even that feels like an effort.

Then, in the furthest possible distance, a tiny purple firework mushroom erupts, and ten seconds later a quiet thump reaches us.

"D'you reckon that's Blackwater Abbas?" he asks.

I sniff. I don't know, but the firework makes me feel better. Warmer. "Let's head that way," I say.

We're now so slow that negotiating our way out of every field seems to take forever. This one doesn't seem to have a way out and I wonder if we've walked in a circle when we clamber over another gate. The ground falls away from us and soon I can hear the river again.

"Oh." Noah slumps to the ground behind me.

"Get up," I say.

"Can't – I've got to eat something," he says.

"There's nothing to eat. We have to keep going."

"Can't I just stay here?"

"No, you can't. Come on, Noah. Get up."

"No," he says.

"Yes," I say. "You have to – you'll die otherwise."

There's a long drawn-out sigh and then I hear him shuffle up alongside me.

Edging our way towards the river I have a sudden notion of where we are. With a little more confidence I march over the squishy grass to a point slightly our side of the river and then slow down, my hands in front of me. "Ow!" I catch my fingers on a barb and follow the wire along in both directions. Wood. A stile.

"Yay," I say, because I know that on the other side of this is a lane – and the lane goes towards the Middle Stoke Airfield, and then Middle Stoke itself. "And Middle Stoke has a pub," I say out loud.

"What?" says Noah.

"A pub, a village with a pub – just a Sunday walk away."

"Really?" says Noah.

"Not far. Don't you remember? The pub by the river, with the playground – that used to do egg and chips."

"I never went there. But ... egg and chips. Oh, no. No – too delicious. I can't bear it."

We have to help each other over the stile. My jeans seem to have fused with my skin, they're so damp. And my rugby shirt is still heavy with water, although the water's kind of warmed up.

The tarmac is pebbly underfoot but at least it doesn't have splinters or thorns and I find I can walk at a reasonable pace. Sanjeev's sock, much like the plastic bags, has no bottom any more. Who knew how badly a rugby sock can wear when it's used as a shoe?

I laugh.

"What's so funny?" asks Noah.

"Rugby socks," I say, not bothering to explain more.

"Oh," he says.

The last glint of sky disappears, and the clouds give a dense black cover, so we have to use the slant of the road to work out the middle.

We walk for ten, fifteen minutes before I hear a car.

"Get in the hedge," I say.

"We could stop them – get a lift," says Noah.

"No," I say. "We can't, in case it's someone we know."

"What? That's mad."

"Trust me, Noah, we need to get off this lane. Hide. Now." And I throw myself through the hedge, brambles and all. I feel Noah's hands behind me and I drag him through too. We land in something soft and wet and smelly. Cowpat?

"Ah!"

"Shhh!" I whisper, as the brakes of the car squeal, feet slap on to the lane and torchlight burns wildly through the pale leaves in the hedgerow.

"What did you see?" says a voice that sounds so like Chris I can't think it's anyone else.

"Prob'ly a rabbit," mutters another. Definitely Dave.

Feet scrape the ground, hands push through the hedge, and then a foot.

Dragging at each other, Noah and I scrabble backwards through more mud and throw ourselves down in a tall patch of nettles. As my legs are stung a thousand times I stifle a scream and peer through my hands back towards the hole in the hedge.

The torch is now very properly on our side. And someone's standing there, playing it slowly across the field.

"See anything?" says the first voice. It's Chris Mumford, and I almost want to run towards him. Safe Chris. He wouldn't hurt us.

Dave has to be the ringleader. Surely.

The torch beam bounces through the undergrowth. From where I am, I can see it very definitely fall on Noah's legs, but perhaps the torch-bearer doesn't expect to find anyone in the nettles.

Boooompffff.

A firework blossoms nearby and something panics in the hedgerow on the other side of the field.

A rabbit.

Shwwwwwweeegh!

Another firework fills the sky. I don't look up, but the torchlight wobbles and the man turns, heading back towards the hole in the hedge.

"Whooooo," I hear Noah exhale.

The torch is switched off. The engine of the vehicle starts and all goes quiet.

Slowly, we uncurl. I've got something smeary down my front, and my skin is tingling from the stinging nettles.

Noah grips my arm and together we help each other across the field to the gap.

"How did you know," he says in the end, "that they weren't looking to help us? That was Dave."

I think about what I heard. Perhaps I've got it all wrong. "And Chris. I'm pretty sure it was Chris. And I don't – not for certain. I really don't. I don't want to believe it either," I say. "I might be completely wrong. But then again. If I'm right..."

Noah lets out an "I don't really believe you but I'll humour you" sigh.

We stay on our own side of the hedge and a pompom of greens and blues bursts into the sky to our left.

"That's not in town. It's too close," he says. "And it's not a proper display."

"Yeah," I say, my feet sliding in something wet and horrible.

At the corner of the field, we squeeze through into the next one. We're now so slow, so cold, we're barely making any progress.

A lone firework blasts into the sky, crackles in a silver cascade, and everything goes quiet. There's just the sound of our feet in the grass, the rapidly freezing grass.

After a long silence, Noah says, "Is the airfield near here?"

"Yeah – before the village."

"There'll be a phone at the airfield."

We struggle on. A vehicle drives slowly along the lane to our right, stops, reverses and comes back again. A door opens, creaks, and slams shut. A second door slams, and there's the rapid breathing sound of a dog. Then there's a torch beam dancing across the tarmac.

Whoever it is combs the hedgerow behind us, muttering to themselves. Or the dog.

"Let's stop," whispers Noah, just as the hedge to our right explodes and something barrels towards us in the dark.

"Dog!" I hiss, stumbling right away from the road towards a dark corner of the field.

Alongside me, Noah's panting, both of us straining for the hedge that has to, needs to, let us through.

Overhead another single firework whooshes into the sky and for a moment everything is lit up. Directly ahead of us is a gap in the hedge, with a wooden bar across. It can't be a stile because there wouldn't be any footpaths over the airfield, but at least it's a way through.

"There!" Noah yells, and the dog growls, its paws crunching across the cold grass, closer, closer. I force my limbs to speed up. Everything hurts – lungs, feet, legs, everything tingles from the nettles. I could just give up.

"Go on, dog," shouts Chris, definitely Chris. "Find 'em."

With a mad burst of energy, I lumber in the dark towards the gap, Noah bumping alongside me, my feet sliding and trampling over so many thistles I could scream.

The fence comes sooner than I imagined and my knees make heavy contact with the wood.

"Ow!"

It's high, with wire netting, and we have to cling to the horizontal rails to get to the top. As I reach the second rung of wood, I feel the dog snapping at my feet. Its teeth grab the remains of the rugby sock. I panic and pull hard. The weight of the dog dangles from my leg until the sock gives up and dissolves, and the dog falls back with a long yowl of defeat.

Above me, Noah hauls on my top to help me over and we tumble in a heap on the far side of the fence. The dog is centimetres away, but unable to get through.

Behind us, the vehicle engine starts up and headlights spring on, shining through the hedge, showing me the whole layout of the entrance to the airfield. At a snail's pace, it creeps forwards. In the field, the dog whines and then begins to bark.

"Now what?" says Noah.

"Shhh," I say, shuffling on hands and knees through the smooth cropped grass of the airfield. The entrance is off to our right; the planes are parked up at the other end. There's about 500 metres of open ground to cross before we get to the first house of the village where a reassuring yellow rectangle of light beams out of an upstairs window. Beyond that, more houses, more lights, more people, and I can even hear voices now.

"C'mon, Noah – houses – not far!" I force my legs one in front of the other, but they're made of jelly and my feet of fire and I can't move as fast as I want to and I keep stumbling and almost falling. Like wind-up toys at the end of their springs we weave across the grass.

"No!" shouts Noah to my left. He hits my arm and points to the right. Through the gate of the airfield bounce a pair of headlights. Too high to be a regular car, and close together, like a Land Rover's. They're slow but they're searching and they're heading towards us.

Far too far in front of us are the cosy windows of houses in the village, but they just aren't moving towards us fast enough. I try to get my legs moving properly. They ache with the effort. "We're not going to make it."

"Left," shouts Noah. "Run to the planes. Dad's plane."

"We should find a phone. What good...?" I pant, but swing to the left, racing down the thin strip of concrete in the middle of the runway, Noah charging along in front of me.

"What?" I shout again.

Behind us, the Land Rover's engine surges as we're spotted by their headlights, and too far ahead, the little group of aircraft clustered at the far end of the runway catch in the leftover beams.

"The red one!" shouts Noah, veering from right to left, and back again.

I follow, my brain briefly registering that Noah has lost all reason, that he thinks we can just steal a plane. I watch as he ducks under a wing, and quite suddenly opens a door on one of the planes.

"Whoa!" My bare feet are slapping across the concrete, burning from the impact. I force myself to sprint until my fingers touch the wing tip. The hot engine of the Land Rover pulls alongside me and the door swings open.

"No you don't!" And I'm yanked back by a hand on the collar of the rugby shirt.

Dave. I struggle to turn. I once watched a film where a woman police officer beats up another officer and in my uncoordinated and frozen way I try to copy her. "Sorry, Dave," I say jabbing my elbow backwards, catching him under the chin, using my other elbow in his ribs, and then knee him, hard. Doubled over, he staggers back and I clutch at the wing, dragging myself forwards towards the plane. Overhead a green firework blossoms and, distracted, I glance up, which gives him the second he needs to lunge for my sleeve.

"Viv!" shouts Noah from the little plane, and suddenly lights come on and the engine sparks into life and the air starts to vibrate.

I pull away from Dave and stagger backwards towards the plane, throwing myself in through the door and slamming it behind me.

"Do up your seat belt."

"What are we doing?" I shout over the clatter of the engine as I struggle with the straps. It's like a really old-fashioned car in here – brown tweed seats, loads of dials, low lights.

"Getting in the air," he shouts back.

"What?" I look around me. There are two seats in the front, and the back's full of boxes. "I thought we were going to use the plane as a car."

Noah shakes his head and we jerk forwards.

Dave's face suddenly jams up against the glass of the door. "Ah!" I scream. Then I undo the little window catch and slip my hand out. "Your own fault!" I say, and jam my fingers into his bearded throat.

"Ow!" He staggers backwards.

"Go," I shout at Noah, and the plane lurches forwards, bouncing over the concrete of the runway. Off to our right there's a figure running. Chris?

Then overhead a firework bursts purple and pink and suddenly we're accelerating along the runway, the figures behind us getting smaller.

Chapter 19

"Can you seriously fly this thing?" I shout.

"Yeah," says Noah after a pause. "No – well, yes. I've kind of done it, loads of times."

And I remember the computer games in his room.

"Flight simulators," I guess.

He nods, and taps one of the dials. "Horizon," he says. Then taps another. "Roll, pitch, yaw – all that."

A new kind of fear grips me. I'm in the hands of a mad person. A person who thinks that a computer game is the same as real life. That flying a plane is no different to flying a computer. Aaaargh.

"Don't do this if you can't do this," I say. "You'll kill us both. People don't survive air crashes. Stop – please – Noah!"

But he ignores me completely, leaning forward, tapping dials, pulling out random knobs, flicking switches and peering through the tiny windscreen. "We used to go on picnics, barbecues – fly to France for an afternoon, all three of us. Back when Dad was more fun."

"Stop, Noah. Don't—"

"And they were happy and we were all happy, and Dad would make fires on the beach with his old petrol lighter and a pile of driftwood."

"STOP!"

"No, Viv. Trust me. Trust me like you used to when we were little – when you rode on the back of my bike."

He doesn't look at me and I don't say that I was terrified all those years ago when we hurtled into the river, me on the back, him steering. That we only did it once. That that was probably the last time we got on with each other. That after that, Daisy became my best friend. That I had gone home and cried and vowed I'd never lose control ever again, that I'd always be boss. That I'd never broken that vow. And here I am again, trusting him with my life. I must be as deluded as he is.

Our lights show the runway stretching ahead. "Perhaps we could turn and get on to the lane."

"Wings," he says. "Wings."

I see what he means. "We could get to the other end of the runway and get out and run."

Suddenly another pair of headlights joins ours.

"Land Rover, on the right," I say.

"OK," says Noah. "Hang on, this might be..." I hear the engine roar, he pushes the steering thing forward and the little plane quivers, bouncing once, twice, and then leaping into the air so that as the Land Rover pulls across to cut us off, we skim over its roof.

"Yay!" I shout.

"We could head for Upper Stanwick – it's the nearest airstrip."

"Plan!" I shout, peering out of the window as we bank around.

Below us small fireworks burst, and the Land Rover appears to park in the middle of a black area that must be the airstrip. We're not exactly soaring, but I don't want to say anything. I can feel Noah's concentration as his hands fly around the various knobs and buttons.

Bang.

Was that a firework?

Bang. Over the sound of the engine I hear another explosion.

"Are they firing at us?" he asks.

We turn and, far too low, whizz back over the runway. I can't see anyone holding a gun – but then I can't see much of anything.

"Why are we doing this?" I say, my hands spread in front of me as if they could possibly prevent certain death. Another pass over the Land Rover gives us an overly close view of two fireworks going off over by the church tower.

Just as the green sparks fall all around us, Noah shouts, "Not high enough to make it over the trees."

"Are we ever going to be high enough?"

He doesn't answer.

"Do we need another plan?"

Again, he doesn't answer, so I undo my seat belt and clamber into the back where the stack of boxes looks promisingly heavy. Pulling open the first pair of flaps, I reach inside and my hand closes around a bottle. I count twelve. And another box of twelve. The box after that is full of something in wrappers, I wrench one open and reach inside. Cheesy snack things. I cram a handful in my mouth and rip the tops off all the others. The next box contains cartons. I can't see the labels but I pull the tag off one and take a glug. Tomato juice. Excellent.

"Can we fly over the Land Rover again!" I shout, holding out a palm full of cheesy snacks that he eats with his tongue like a cat.

"Seriously?" yelps Noah, but he swings us around surprisingly steadily at the end of the aerodrome so that we get a brief, overly close-up view of the church tower, backlit by fireworks. As we head back over the airfield, I see the Land Rover standing in the middle of the runway and one of the figures, a big figure, Chris, silhouetted by the headlights.

The fireworks are really kicking off now, popping up from the village in mushroom bursts every few seconds.

Bang.

Another far-too-close firework goes off and I can't help but jump as the sparks fall all around us.

Beside me, Noah jerks, whisking the plane to the left, and we lurch, and I hear something scrape on the underside of the fuselage.

"Trees!" he shouts, wobbling around them, but not getting any higher.

Now I understand why we're flying back and forth along the airstrip, he doesn't *know* how to get any higher.

"Head for the hangars. Try and circle there!" I shout. The hangars are near the entrance to the airfield. There's an old control tower there, which Mum and I used to pretend was haunted because sometimes there were lights even though it's been locked up for years. We make an unsteady circle, our altitude increasing a little, and I watch as the Land Rover glides up the runway in our direction.

"Fly over it," I shout.

"Why?" yells Noah.

"Just do it," I say.

We break from the circle and I load the bottom of the little opening window next to me with four pristine boxes of tomato juice, a bunch of cheese snacks and a single bottle wedged in the open gap.

"Now!" I shout at myself and hit my forearm down on the window. Everything disappears and I just hope it's made contact in the right places as I load it up again. Tomato juice, snacks, unknown bottles. This time higher and, as Noah banks, I send it flying, getting the tiny satisfaction of seeing a tomato juice splat on to the concrete right in front of the Land Rover's headlights.

One of the figures runs with their hand over their head towards the shelter of the Land Rover.

They don't like it, but tomato juice is not going to make them go away. We're going to need something more than drinks mixers.

For a moment, the engine seems to cut out, and then restart. We lurch, but I don't particularly think about it: I'm too busy watching the ground. From time to time I get glimpses of people over by the church, watching the fireworks, and then I spot the Land Rover and it all whizzes past again, sickeningly fast.

I load the window a third time and Noah shouts, tapping at something in front of him.

"Fuel!" is the only word I catch.

I peer over his shoulder. The fuel gauge is at empty. "Did you check it when you took off?"

"It's old," he shouts. "Dad was having it fixed."

And then I realise what he means. We're in an ancient aircraft and we've sprung a leak. Of course we have. I imagine the long trail of aircraft gasoline connecting us to the airfield. Really easy to light. Really quick to explode.

"Don't go anywhere near the fireworks," I shout, and he nods. I'm sure he's worked that one out himself.

The engine stops and starts again. We lose a little height, and my stomach lurches.

"Are we going to crash?" I ask.

"If I can just get it to work – there's an auxiliary tank," he shouts.

"What? A second one?"

He nods. "Dad had it put in so that we could fly to France," he shouts. "Just hope there's something in it."

I watch the gauge go into the red, hear the engine sputter and we stop-start, falling and rising and jerking across the field.

"Come on, Noah, switch it on!" I shout.

"Just using every drop," he says, and the little propeller in front of us stops turning.

"Are you mad!" I shout and Noah flips a switch, and the gauge jumps up to a quarter full.

Wow. We soar away from the runway, the fireworks well below us again. I peer backwards towards the two figures by the control tower. Their Land Rover is parked at the bottom, blocking the runway. Even if we landed now, they'd get us. I imagine that's what they're waiting for. And it doesn't look to me as if we're going to land anywhere else. Noah doesn't know how to do anything more than bumble back and forth. We have to get them out of the way – we have to stop them ourselves or we have to bring the police.

But the trail of fuel that we must have left gives me an idea. A dangerous idea, but an idea all the same. I reach into the boxes. The lids of the bottles unscrew surprisingly easily and I sniff. It practically takes the skin off the back of my throat. I don't know what it is, but it's really strong, really flammable.

"Do you think the first tank's empty?" I shout.

He nods.

"Do you think we could still catch fire?"

He shakes his head.

Next to the control tower is a wooden hut. It's got a roof, but I don't think it's much of a roof. Fires on airfields must bring fire engines, surely.

If we could just start one.

Frantically, I search the thing that I would call a glove compartment. There's all sorts of old rubbish, sweet wrappers and maps and bits of paper and eventually I find what I'm looking for. *And Dad would make fires on the beach with his old petrol lighter.* An old petrol lighter, with a flint and a wheel like Connor uses for lighting the bonfires. They don't go out when you let go of them. You have to close the lid to extinguish the flame.

"When I say 'go', fly to the other end of the strip!" I shout. I drop twelve bottles of the spirit out of the window in a continuous stream until I'm sure that several of them have gone through the roof of the shed.

And then I spin the wheel of the lighter. Sparks fly, but nothing else happens.

"No!" I cry, and then I spin it again.

And again.

And again.

Ping. A wobbly flame springs into the square.

"Whatever you're doing, do it quickly," shouts Noah. "We can't stay up here for ever!"

I place the lighter, lit, in a Ritz cracker box with some paper from the glove compartment, and a bottle of the spirit and jam it through the window. I'm either killing us or saving us.

"Go! Go! Go!"

And I drop it – the box's sides reflecting the lights of the car, falling, falling, and disappearing in through the hole in the roof of the shed.

"Yesssss…!"

We fly on, and I look back at the darkness, at the men standing by the control tower, and I hope that the shed is full of paper, or old furniture or petrol or something that'll light. As we pass back, I look down and for a moment it's all horribly black, but then a small ball of orange bursts where the shed must be and within seconds the roof is a silhouette, with fire behind. I watch transfixed as the orange advances along the structure of the shed.

Then, there's a puff, and smoke blocks the view, and a satisfying column of sparks rise from the walls as growing flames leap across the concrete, presumably finding the previous bottles of spirit. They illuminate the tower, the Land Rover, the men and the whole airstrip.

"God, Viv!" shouts Noah. "We'll be roasted – the fuel."

"You said it would be OK." I swallow. "We'll be all right, won't we?"

Suddenly the plane bumps and Noah's head swings forward and he bangs his nose on the steering wheel thingy. "Arrgh!" he shouts, and blood bursts from his nose. "Ow!" He takes both hands and clamps them over his face.

"Noah!" I shout. We head straight into darkness. "Noah?"

I clamber back into the front and stare at the instruments. There's one that looks like a horizon and then a bunch of others.

Grabbing a mangy blanket from the back, I cram it over his face and grab the steering thing, pointing it upwards. A flag suddenly comes into view on my right and I realise we must be directly over the village. I spare a second and look down. I can actually see the roofs of houses and people pointing up at us.

"Oh, god," I mutter and pull the plane back round so that we're heading for the fire by the control tower. Blue lights are racing down the lane – police? Fire? Brilliant – but they're on the ground and I'm in an aeroplane.

"Noah, what do I do?" I shout. "How do I land this thing?"

"I don't know," he says through the blanket.

"You mean you really don't know or you don't know right now because your nose is spouting all over the cabin?"

He shakes his head. "I really don't," he mumbles.

"You mean you've never done it?"

"No," he says. "No – when I play games, I usually crash."

For the second time in ten minutes, fear almost paralyses me.

"So I've as much chance as you do?" I say.

He groans next to me and I wonder if he's passed out.

I set the wheel so that it's pointing forwards, over the bonfire, towards the flat of the river. "Wake up, Noah. Wake up!"

He groans.

I can't reach all the buttons. "Noah!"

But he's slumped there, leaden, not moving at all.

"Oh, for god's sake!" I cry, tugging at him.

He stirs.

"Get out of the seat!" I say, bashing him, pulling him to the side.

He stirs and shuffles awkwardly, falling backwards into the space behind. I scramble over his legs until I cram myself into his seat. The pilot's seat.

"What do these pedals do?" I say, trying them. The plane dips from side to side and I realise I should just leave them alone.

"Noah, wake up!" I yell, holding the plane steady and trying to ease it up higher, out of the way of the fireworks, and the trees, which I can't see.

Blue lights appear, chasing across the landscape.

"Noah!" I shout. "Wake up!"

Without meaning to I tilt the plane and we go into a long turn until we seem to be pointing back the way we came. I'm not sure, but at least we have some fuel and I seem to be able to keep us up off the ground.

"Viv!" he mutters at last, and clambers forward until he's sitting in my seat. "Sorry – I passed out."

"Yeah, yeah – I got that," I say, pushing the stick thing forward and getting a little height. I try moving it a little to the left, and a little to the right. We tip noticeably, and the fire swings across the windscreen.

"Speed's important!" he shouts.

I glance at him. Admittedly he's lit only by the dashboard lights but he's totally white, except where he's covered in blood.

The blue lights are now clustered around the control tower. Clouds of smoke are rising from the fire and drift across us. "Think it's safe to land?" I shout and slowly I swing the plane around, keeping the control tower on our right, and so that the runway stretches ahead towards the parked planes at the far end.

I let the wind speed drop. I've no idea what speed I should be going, but I imagine something like sixty miles an hour would be OK – Mum drives at sixty miles an hour.

"Too slow!" shouts Noah as the speed reaches seventy-nine and he points to something like a bath plug on the dashboard. "You really can't go below eighty."

"Eighty?" I think of Mum on the motorway. She says eighty is too fast. "Really?"

"Trust me," he says.

Trust me.

"Thought you'd never landed!" I say, pulling the plug thing and suddenly shooting forward.

"You'll just drop from the sky!"

I pull it more and the little engine surges.

"Too fast! Go up, go up!" I shove on the steering thing and we shoot up into the black. All I can see is night and without the horizon thingy I wouldn't be able to work this out at all. The engine screams then for one terrifying second sputters before restarting.

"Height!" he shouts, and I look at the dial. I don't understand what it says, but I pull back on the steering thing and we go up more gently so that I can actually turn the plane until we're pointing towards the blue lights, speeding back towards the control tower. I just hope there are no trees underneath us.

Crack. A twig hits the windscreen.

OK, so there were trees, but luckily the plane keeps going, and I look at a height thing that must be telling us how high above the ground we are.

Nothing's swaying, the wings feel steady and I let the speed go down, ninety, eighty-five...

"Too slow," shouts Noah.

I don't care any more. People survive car crashes at seventy miles an hour. Don't they?

The blue lights are almost at our eye height – the ground's coming up towards us, the airstrip appearing in our headlights, a thin black line of tar running down the middle in front of us. I lock on to it, keeping it straight in front, and I let the speed drop.

Bump.

We bounce. I bite my tongue.

Bump.

The front tips forward, my neck jerks, then we're in the air, then back on the ground again.

"Pedals! Brakes!" yells Noah, throwing himself and the bloody rugby shirt across my lap and pulling on a lever I'd never noticed.

We slew to the right, skid to the left and then, centimetres from a fire engine, incredibly, we stop.

Chapter 20

We're both shaking when the policeman opens the door and looks inside.

"Ruddy hell!" he says, and then turns and shouts into the darkness. "Sarge – over here!"

* * *

They bundle us into a police car. With hot chocolate that appears from nowhere and biscuits and blankets.

A paramedic checks my feet. Checks Noah's bite.

No one says anything much and it feels like a dream. Next to me, blood-encrusted Noah makes gurgling noises and I would just fall asleep but outside a policewoman's talking into a radio and I'm listening.

"Yes, we've got them disarmed and cuffed, bringing them all in just as soon as the exit's cleared, sir. Yes, one of them's caught a nasty crack to his head, so the medics are keeping him under observation."

Tinny sounds come back through her receiver.

"Yes – absolutely, sir. His father's plane, seems he knew where the keys were kept, under the wing. Yes, sir, not very secure – will do. Intact, but he's got a dog bite. Have you informed the parents?"

Another siren screams and an ambulance stops in front of the police car. Through the windscreen I see a body on a stretcher, an arm hanging over the side.

Pale-pink skin shows in the headlights.

Dave. It's Dave. A nasty crack?

She talks into her radio and I sink back on the seat, watching as the ambulance crew load Dave into the back. There's blood. He looks as if he's been in an accident.

Fireworks bang over our heads, cracking and whizzing, and distantly someone plays a piece of classical music through some dodgy speakers.

I pull the blanket around my shoulders and sip at my hot chocolate. It's all for the police to do now. I can fall asleep. My eyes close, the sounds begin to blur, my body relaxes. My feet throb.

"What the—? Ow!"

Next to me, Noah has thrown his hot chocolate into the air. It lands all over my leg.

"Ow – Noah – ow! You idiot!" I shout, scuttling backwards along the seat.

In less than a second we're surrounded. Black police jackets, handcuffs, a stretcher, green men in ambulance gear.

"It was just my hot chocolate," says Noah, looking up into all the faces. "Sorry. Sorry, Viv."

And I sit back on my bum on the warm wet seat, and for the first time, I let myself cry.

Chapter 21

While they mop up the hot chocolate they sit us in the boot of a paramedic's car, our legs hanging over the side. The fireworks are still crackling and banging overhead, and they're kind of pretty, but I don't think they'll ever be quite as wonderful for me after tonight. Witnessing them close up through the windows of the little aircraft was too scary.

Landing that plane was terrifying.

From here I can see Chris, his big shoulders sagging, on a chair, a paramedic working at something on his foot. He looks exhausted, defeated, and looking at him makes me feel angry.

All that fury I had with Noah, and his father and everyone. All that stuff that meant that Mum was taken away, and I was shouted at and we nearly drowned, and we were shot at – and it was them all the time.

I blink back angry tears but they won't stop, it's like someone's left the tap running. But eventually they run out, and I'm left sniffing in the darkness, trying to make sense of it all.

Time passes. An age. What are we waiting for? They've wrapped us in space blankets, and people in green keep on taking measurements and temperatures and checking stuff. They've bandaged Noah's dog bite and muttered about rabies injections but they don't look worried.

"Would you like a custard cream?" says the policewoman who took my phone all that time ago. I resist saying something really rude and shake my head. I'm kind of losing interest in biscuits. She's wearing her dayglo again, but she looks more comfortable here in the middle of the blue flashing lights. I glance over to Noah. He's staring at the wreckage of a packet of cheesy crackers, but I don't think he's thinking about food. Between us and Chris are three policemen wearing full body armour. I think at least one of them has a gun.

I kind of hope that they do.

As if she can read my thoughts the dayglo policewoman puts down her mug and says, "If you're wondering, Chris Mumford is being held here because we can't get him out until another vehicle arrives." She gives me a tight smile. "We don't want to take you in the same one. Sorry about that. Won't be much longer."

I close my eyes for a second and imagine the flooded countryside. It must stretch for miles. Everything would take ages to get here.

A car pulls on to the runway and Inspector Hager arrives. The dayglo policewoman rushes to report something but the inspector walks over to us and leans quietly against the car.

"How are you both?" she asks.

I think about all the finer details. "OK," I say in the end, and Noah nods.

Across the concrete Chris shouts and the paramedic steps back and the armed policemen step forward.

"So you can identify both of these men?" says Inspector Hager, ignoring the shouts.

I nod.

"Dave McAndrew, Chris Mumford," says Noah.

"Why was Dave on the stretcher?" I ask.

"Hit on the head with a bottle. It seems to have come from an aeroplane," says the dayglo detective.

"Oh!" I say, a complicated set of thoughts racing through my head.

"He'll be OK," says Inspector Hager. "Can I ask if you think there were any more people involved – should we be interviewing anyone else at this stage?"

She opens a tube of mints and flicks one into her mouth.

I wonder about the big piles of holiday brochures in Chris's girlfriend Sharon's car. "Sharon? Chris's girlfriend – she might have known. They probably wanted the money," I say, twisting a strand of hair around my finger. Closing my eyes I run through all the others on the estate. All the people I've trusted. Tony? Shona? Connor? Pavel? Natalia and Olga? Maria? They surely wouldn't be involved, but then I'd never have thought Chris or Dave would – I struggle to find the word in my head – betray us like this. How could they do it? "I dunno," I mutter. "I haven't a clue."

I think back to the summers spent wandering the

estate. All those years with them, did what we were told, followed them, learned from them.

"How could they?" I say out loud.

"Sorry?" says Inspector Hager, and Noah nods.

"I know what you mean," he says. "I've known them all my life."

From the biscuit debris beside me, I take an almost complete custard cream and nibble at it.

"Oh!" Inspector Hager turns.

I drop my biscuit.

Chris has started shuffling across the concrete towards us. His hands are in handcuffs and the blue lights flick across his face.

Noah backs into the car, but I stand on my bound feet and limp towards him just as he limps towards me.

"Vivienne," warns Inspector Hager.

I hold up my hand. I can handle this – I want to handle this. I'm not just going to sit in a car and feel sorry for myself. I want to know why.

"I'm sorry," says Chris.

I don't say anything.

"I'm sorry about all of it – for both of you. I'm sorry I took you, boy. It was supposed to be simple, easy."

"But you could have killed us, Chris." I speak loudly, clearly. I want everyone to hear this. "You nearly did. And what about Sanjeev. We found blood..."

He lets out a long sigh. "It went wrong. He tried to be a hero, stepped out in front of the van. So we stopped and then he jumped me and we fought – the gun went off..."

"Oh," I say. Anger or sadness? I can't work it out.

I control my breathing and wait the longest time before I ask, "Why, Chris – why did you do it? Why did you do any of it?"

He sniffs and looks across at Noah. He tilts his head from side to side and I decide he's trying to work out whether to say something or not.

Inspector Hager looks off to the left and, as if on cue, a police car screams into the airfield and three figures race across the concrete, a fourth walking slowly behind. It's Lady B and Tai and—

"Mum!" I shout as she and Tai hurtle towards me. Tai's skipping from side to side, yipping and yapping. "Mum."

"Oh, my god! Viv," she says, throwing her arms into a hug, clutching me. We cling to each other, our arms interlocking. Alongside us Lady B lands in a cloud of perfume and enfolds Noah and I hear his snuffly tears as he hugs her back. "My poor little darling."

"Mum, Mum," he mumbles.

Tai leaps into my arms and licks my face, and I nuzzle his grizzled coat. "Tai, Mum." We all hug, closer and closer.

I gradually realise that Chris is laughing. It's a hollow laugh. "Don't hug her – she's a liar," he shouts.

What does he mean? I look at Mum and she looks confused.

"She made us do it. *Her*." He points with a handcuffed arm right at Lady Belcombe.

"Me?" she laughs. "Me? Why would I kidnap my own son? What on earth...?"

Inspector Hager stands quite still, listening, while the dayglo detective is recording everything on a proper camera.

A deep voice sounds in the shadows and Lord B steps forward. "Julia?" he asks.

"Why are you all staring at me?" says Lady Belcombe, her eyes wide, her hands up in front of her as if she can push us all back. "I haven't done anything. It's him – all him. He's the one you should be accusing." She points back at Chris, who glares at her.

"You needed the money, didn't you, Lady Belcombe?" he says. "Gambling got a bit out of control, didn't it? And when your loan shark came calling, you got desperate."

"Gambling?" says Lord B. "I thought ... I thought you'd given that up, Julia? I thought that was all in the past? You said—"

Chris interrupts him. "Lot of money your good lady wife owes."

Lady B reaches for the side of the car, as if she's going to collapse. Her mouth keeps opening and closing but she doesn't say anything.

"Mum?" says Noah, silver tears tracing down his cheek. "I don't understand."

"Lady Belcombe?" Inspector Hager prompts.

"Noah – I'm – I'm so," Lady Belcombe wipes her face with the back of her hand. "I – I – thought it wouldn't hurt..." She tries to snuggle between us but Noah pushes her arms aside as she attempts to hug him. "Please, darling – please." He shoves her away with his feet, and backs himself further into the boot of the car. "You had me kidnapped?" he shouts. "You had me kidnapped!"

Lord B is talking but I'm not sure anyone's really listening. I think he's trying to explain it to himself. "But this can't possibly be true – I'll speak to the Chief Constable. Preposterous! There must be some sort of ridiculous mistake. Julia? Julia?" Taking her place he sits down next to Noah. "What are they saying? Surely it was Mumford – this man who we trusted…" He falls silent as the inspector raises her hand and then he says again, "I don't understand."

"Oh, for god's sake, you idiotic man. Shut up and listen!" Lady B interrupts, her voice sharp but on the edge of breaking. "I couldn't ask. I couldn't. I was too ashamed – and anyway, I don't think you'd have given me the money. Peregrine certainly wouldn't. So I came up with this. It was all going to be so easy, so simple. I knew you and Peregrine would pay up for Noah; he's the last beastly Belcombe after all, your precious child… But it got out of control because of that fool."

I'm not sure if she means Chris or Sanjeev, but her husband stares at her as if he's never seen her before.

"Poor Sanjeev," whispers Mum, sniffing. "He was in the car." The sides of her mouth go down.

"Car?" I mutter, thinking of the Mini.

"The old one in the dump."

"What?"

"Shhhh – tell you later."

"And you?" says Inspector Hager, facing Chris, and I realise all this is staged. We're all here so that we can ask the right questions – Lord B, Chris, Lady B, us. "Why?"

Chris looks at the ground. "It was the Newbury job I did, back in '88. A security guard was killed. I was nineteen. I was holding the gun. I didn't mean to but..." He looks up at Lady B. "She knew. She found out, dug around in my past – got a confession from some bloke in a pub. She used it against me. She blackmailed me. I was going to lose everything – my job, house, everything. Dave helped, cos he's a mate, but I should never have dragged him into it." Chris swallows.

Lady B's arms hang loosely by her sides. She swings them slightly and then, without warning, grabs a small fire extinguisher from the back of the car and races towards Chris, her elbow jabbing back, flinging the cylinder towards his head. "You utter idiot. You imbecile, you've destroyed everything!" she shouts, just as both the armed policemen jump on her and crash to the ground.

* * *

Hours later, sitting in the hall with Tai at my feet, Mum on the sofa next to me and Lord B next to Noah with arms clamped around his son as if he could suddenly fill with helium and float away, we get properly warm. About every five minutes Lord B squeezes Noah, crushing him with love. "Noah, Noah, my boy, my lovely boy, I thought I'd never see you again."

"Dad," says Noah, his head jammed up in the crook of his father's neck, silver tears trailing down his face. "Dad." After the fifth time, Lord B reaches across and envelops me too in a clumsy, scratchy embrace, his half-beard tickling the top of my forehead, his arms holding me as tight as he held Noah. "Viv," he mutters. "Viv, thank you. Thank you."

It would be awkward – but so much has happened today that I can't find anything embarrassing any more and it feels like a moment of intense reality that I might remember for the rest of my life.

I look across. They sit together, so close that Noah's blond curls mix with his father's darker, greyer mane, and I wonder if I've ever seen them actually embrace like this. Father and son. Reaching towards each other, entwined. Loving.

The firelight dances across their faces, both staring into the flames.

The police have gone. They've stopped asking questions. We know that Sanjeev is dead, and that he died being a hero. We know that they kept his body in the old car in the dump. It must have been there both times I visited. I shiver. I'm glad I didn't see him, find him.

And in spite of the fact that I still kind of loathe him, I'm actually sad for Noah. He's lost his mother and he'll probably never be able to forgive her.

"Things are going to have to change round here," says Lord B quietly. "New beginnings," he says to the fire.

I wonder what he means. Quite a lot is going to change – quite a lot already has changed. Nothing about the Blackwater Estate is how it was a week ago. I twiddle my toes, which are covered in white cream and wrapped in weird cotton sock things. "No lasting harm," the paramedic had said as she trussed them up. I've got them resting on a leather pouffe thingy that probably cost a thousand pounds, but no one seems to mind. No one seems to mind about anything. Tai's chewing some disgusting fake bone thing that Mum bought him. We've eaten cheese on toast in our pyjamas and scattered crumbs all over the place and no one made us sit at the table.

"Does that mean…?" Noah begins, and then stops.

"What, my boy?" says his father, gazing into the fire and stroking Noah's curls.

Tai drops his chew and rests his head on my knee. Tigger looks disgusted and clambers up to sleep on the back of a chair.

Noah swallows. "Does that mean I can change schools?"

A frown casts a shadow over Lord B's face. "But you're doing so well at St David's? Aren't you? Friends and that sort of thing."

Noah shakes his father's hands out of his hair. "No, Dad, I'm not. I don't." He looks at his feet. "Actually, Dad, I don't really have any friends."

"Oh, Noah, that can't be true." Lord B strokes him, like he's a dog. "You must have lots of friends. What about that tall boy, MP's son, was it? Didn't you go to his party?"

Noah nods his head. "I did. And they ended up

burying me in leaves, if you remember – he and the rest of the rugby team."

Lord B frowns. "How about that chap from Germany, what was his name? Hans? Helmut? Father ran a bank or something."

"He was called Harald and he left after a week. He hated the place."

"But St David's is such a good school. I went there, Peregrine went there – and your grandfather. It's … a tradition. And people go to such good universities. Everyone's so clever."

Noah sighs. "Dad, could I just change schools?" he says. "Go somewhere like – Herschel High?"

Lord B looks shocked. Mum drops her glasses on the floor.

"But that's my school," I say slowly. "You want to go to my school? It's not like St David's – not at all."

"Exactly," says Noah. "Please, Dad? I just want friends – ordinary friends. People who do ordinary things. No one does ordinary things at St David's. All their parents are members of parliament or live in South America. No one just … hangs out, like Viv does with her friends."

"Oh, I don't know," says Lord B, looking across

at Mum as if she might know the answer. "No Belcombe has ever been to school anywhere else."

Mum prods me.

I glance up at her.

She whispers, "Come on, Viv."

For a second I feel doubtful. Noah? Herschel High? Then I think of all the people that go there – every kind of person. Then I realise that the idea of seeing more of Noah actually makes me smile and then I say, "Do you want to come to the Christmas market with me and the gang?" It comes out of my mouth before I've even properly thought about it.

Noah's face lights up. "Really?"

I nod. "Really, yes." I examine my feelings. "Although, you have to promise that you won't be Viscount whatnot, that you'll just be Noah."

He glares at me.

"That's very kind of you," he says, all formally. "And I'd like to take you up on your offer, but you must promise that you won't call me inbred, or a tadpole, or a school dinner, or anything like that."

Lord B raises an eyebrow. Mum goes red.

I probably go red too.

"Deal – if you promise not to *be* a complete

tadpole."

Noah's smile broadens. His face cracks with the glow. "God, Viv – I'd like that – I'd like that more than anything."

And I look up at his dad and my mum and I see that their smiles are as large as his and I feel, deep inside, a door opening to a giant smile of my own.